A DEATH IN THE FAMILY

Other titles published by EPRINT Publishing

A Measure of the Soul by Stephanie Baudet
Missing Link by Elizabeth Kay
Spectacles by Pippa Goodhart
This Fragile Life by David Webb

About the author:

Caroline Dunford lives in Scotland with her partner and two young sons. When she isn't attending to the whims of the men in her life she writes short stories, plays, novels, non-fiction and the occasional article. As all authors are required to have as much life experience as possible she has, at various times, been a drama-coach, an archery instructor, a counsellor, a qualified psychotherapist, a charity worker, a journalist, a voice actor, a hypnotherapist and a playwright. While accepting life will always throw many and varied challenges at all of us she believes a sense of humour remains the most effective shield against the trials and tribulations of life.

A DEATH IN THE FAMILY

A Euphemia Martins Mystery

Caroline Dunford

PRINT
PUBLISHING

Published in Great Britain in 2009 by EPRINT Publishing
Blackburn, Lancashire
www.eprint.co.uk

© Caroline Dunford 2009

A CIP record for this work is available from the British Library.
ISBN 978-1-905637-90-4

Typeset in Great Britain by Educational Printing Services Limited,
Blackburn, Lancashire
Printed and bound in Great Britain by CPI Cox & Wyman,
Reading, Berkshire

For the boys, M and X, who are in equal parts inspiring and distracting, but always wonderful, and for Graham, without whom so much would not have been possible.

Serious Consequences

In December 1909, England was gearing up for a General Election, Russia was rumbling with the undercurrent of revolution, and my father, the very Reverend Joshia Peter Martins expired, face down, in his dish of mutton and onions leaving Mother, myself and my little brother Joe at the whim of Bishop Pagget.

Quite in character, Mother was more concerned with the immediate rather than long term consequences. "Why did he not call for the dishes to be removed before port!" she had cried when our housekeeper had summoned us to the fateful table. "To be found among such common fare. Oh Joshia!" As it was rare for her to use his Christian name, I immediately realised this was my mother in deep despair.

"He looks very peaceful," I offered tactfully. In fact, my father looked if anything, deeply relieved. He had the aspect of a man who had welcomed death, albeit he had found it among the gravy, and this helped me bear the awful, wrenching pain I felt at his loss.

"Oh, Euphemia, if only your father . . ."

"There was really nothing he could do about it," I countered fairly.

My mother lifted a haughty eyebrow at me. "Do not interrupt, young lady. It is not at all becoming. I was going to say if only your father had not been a vicar."

"I'm sure he didn't take the decision lightly, Mother."

"I have no way of knowing. It was before he met me," Mother paused and then shook her head. "It really will not do. I will write to your grandfather."

"I will be only too delighted if he offers to help us, but you have been writing to that man for most of my life, Mother, and he has never bothered to reply."

"He is not 'that man', Euphemia. He is your grandfather."

"He has never behaved as one," I declared, grief lending my tone a sharpness I did not intend.

"Just like your father," snapped my mother

and left.

Despite my glossy, abundant chestnut hair and clear, grey intelligent eyes, I fear at eighteen I am not, nor ever will be, my mother's ideal of a good daughter. Between us lay the "not inconsiderable hours" I had spent at Pa's side in his study, while he taught me what he could of the world, how to think analytically and what little he had grown to understand of the human soul during his time as a man of the cloth. My mother considered intelligence "as much use on a young girl as a pair of hooves and about as attractive". I once pointed out how this could occasion a very great saving on shoes and Pa had to stand by as I was sent to bed without supper. Mother and Pa were not close, but without Pa all our futures were dangerously uncertain.

As a widow, neither traditionally beautiful nor having a fashionable simpering personality, my mother was of little interest to Bishop Pagget. The eviction letter was sent by his secretary the day after my father's death.

So while Mother retired to her room to grieve and continue her one-sided correspondence with my grandfather, I took decisive action. I began to write letters of my own to various country houses. I cannot say where the idea came from. It was certainly born of desperation, but I confess at this point it appealed to my sense of romanticism which I have failed to repress despite witnessing the outcome of my parents' love-match. But when one is named after a young virgin martyr, who was mauled to death by bears for refusing to make pagan sacrifices, I feel one is entitled to a little whimsy in one's nature.

Naturally, I took precautions to protect my identity. I directed all answers to the nearby post office and chose a *nom-de-plume*. I told the postmistress I was collecting letters for my cousin, who was to join us shortly. This blatant falsehood cost me some sleep, but I doubted anything would transpire of the scheme.

So, I was somewhat taken aback when, after a flood of rejections, I received a positive reply. How on earth would I tell Mother?

As it happened, it was Little Joe who let my secret out of the bag. I was in my room thinking of what I would take with me, when Little Joe barrelled through the door and bolted under the bed. "I'm sorry, Effie," he called, "I didn't mean to give you away."

My mother's voice rose up through the hall. "Euphemia Martins, come downstairs at once!"

I bent down and looked under the bed. My brother scuttled backwards with the speed of a spider escaping a broom. "Joe, what have you done?"

"I didn't mean to. Mother kept going on

about what were we to do and how you weren't any help hiding in your room. I didn't think it was fair, so I might have let slip about your great adventure."

"Great adventure?"

"I found one of your letters. I think it's a grand idea, Effie. You could meet a rich nobleman and he could fall in love with you and give you jewels and a great house and no one deserves it more than you, Effie. You're quite pretty, you know, for a sister. Maybe you'd even be able to buy me the wooden soldier set Pa had promised me for my birthday."

"Oh Joe! You had no business . . ."

I heard our creaky stairs moan under the approaching weight of my mother, resplendent in her heavy widow's weeds.

Mother arrived at my door and paused, dark and looming, on the threshold to make an impression. Mother retains the hereditary ability to make her presence felt despite being a mere whisker over four feet ten inches.

"Euphemia, I will not countenance such disgrace."

At her tone Little Joe edged further under my bed.

"We need to eat, Mother."

"Euphemia! A young girl knows nothing of such things."

"Mother, we all get hungry. Especially Little Joe."

Mother hesitated. Little Joe helpfully popped his angelic, curly topped features out from under the bed. Mother heaved a great sigh and folded herself down onto the mattress like some giant black velvet despairing fan. "It's not as if I will be using my real name," I offered. "And you do have to leave the vicarage. I can help with the rent as well as Joe's schooling."

Joe pulled a face at me.

"If Grandfather doesn't reply," I began, "we have to leave here in two weeks."

Mother turned on her heel, calling for Joe to come practise his Latin, and left without a backward glance. She knew as well as I how desperate our situation was becoming.

I did not believe that Grandfather would come to our aid, but I hoped. Surely, even by his unreasonable standards, Mother had paid for her crime. I could not believe the old man would not at least acknowledge his grandson. It seemed positively medieval. But as the days turned into a week it became clear I was more of a romantic than my grandfather.

I confess I even dug out my *Morte D'Arthur*. My parents had taught me that romantic love does not fare well in the real world, but for a few sleepless nights I could not help but harbour fantasies that my white knight would arrive and rescue us all. (Even my healthy imagination could not conjure up the image of my mother inspiring a young knight, so although it was in many ways against my principles I was prepared to be the damsel in distress.)

A week later no white knight had appeared. Neither was there any letter. My mother's face closed in upon itself and Little Joe, try as he might, could not conjure up antics to make her smile. Instead she threw herself into the business of packing. Finally, she took up the household reins once more and began to make inquiries no lady should ever have to make – concerning cottages for rent. I, in my turn, made my decision and wrote the letter that would seal my future. As I penned my acceptance, I had never felt better named. At least I could be fairly certain the Staplefords did not keep bears.

Mother and I avoided each other. In our blacks we flitted round the house like ghosts in some macabre waltz, partnered in grief and the tasks of shutting up the house, draping long white sheets over furniture and possessions we had once considered ours, each of us silently contemplating our separate fates. If only she had been less reserved, less closed with me, our grief might have brought us closer together, but the only affection I ever saw her willingly display was towards Little Joe. To be fair my younger brother has the sweetest of natures and the most endearing, engaging smile, it would be an impossibility for any woman not to love him and any man not to want to tousle his locks and give him a penny; a skill he might need to employ in the near future if I did not follow through with my plan.

So, early one spring morning, Mother and I met each other in the hallway, each of us with our own serious news. As usual Mother went first.

"I have found a cottage, Euphemia. It will not be what we are used to, but it is small and neat with a yard for chickens and space for two pigs and a goat. I believe goat's milk to be most nutritious. I have taken it on a three months term and we will take possession next Tuesday. I have made inquiries in the village and have already gained four students for the pianoforte. I expect the number to rise once I am established. Of course, I will have to continue Little Joe's education myself, but I hope in time we will again be able to afford a tutor. Perhaps you would be so kind as to select from your father's study the books you feel will be most suitable?"

I had some idea of what this request had cost her. "Does Bishop Pagget not require a full inventory?"

My mother had the grace to blush as she

replied, "We will adjust it accordingly."

I had no problem of depriving the old Port-and-Bluster (as my father had called him), but I was surprised at my mother's decision. It must have showed in my face.

"Really, Euphemia, you are usually more than ready to flout convention!"

Now was the time to tell her. I could not find the words. Instead, I stepped aside and revealed my bag, standing behind me, packed full of all I could not bear to leave behind me. My mother's hand stole to her mouth. "You haven't," she gasped.

"I am sorry, Mother. I have taken a position at Stapleford Hall." I half expected a dramatic declaration that I was no longer her daughter. Her reaction took me by complete surprise.

My mother embraced me. "I'm sorry," she whispered so softly I could not be sure of the words. Then she stepped back and said, much in her normal manner, "I hope it is at least a senior maid. It would be ridiculous for you to give up all your chances to earn no more than I shall be paying 'a girl that does.'"

"I will be a maid with upstairs responsibilities."

My mother made a most unladylike noise. "Stapleford Hall. Aping the great houses."

"I think that's why they have taken me. I have

no references. But I am intelligent and I have hope my employer will notice this. I intend to rise to the position of housekeeper quite swiftly."

Mother sighed. "You are very naïve, Euphemia. Fortunately I shall not be far away when you find yourself evicted from the house. The cottage is in Little Crosshore. You will always have a place with Little Joe and I," Mother said grandly, although at this point we both knew that it would be nigh on impossible for her to maintain the rent on a property as she had described without help from my wages. I didn't think she would make the most popular of music teachers.

"I will return home to visit whenever my employers allow."

"Whenever your employers allow? Never did I think to hear a daughter of mine utter such words."

I judged it time to make a sharp exit; Mother was growing dramatic. I assured her Stapleford Hall had arranged for a carrier to pick me up at the square – yet more lamentations, "a common carrier". I kissed Little Joe goodbye and promised him his soldiers. Then I stepped out into the bright morning of 8th January 1910, and prepared to leave behind me not only my old life, but my name. The air was sharp as lemon on my skin and the wind whipped a tear into my eyes, but more than any other emotion, I am ashamed to say, the one that was uppermost in my heart as I left my childhood home behind was excitement; excitement at this new beginning.

My excitement was slightly dampened both literally and figuratively by the storm that opened over me that day. It took the carrier longer than he expected to get the old cart down increasingly muddy lanes, but as the afternoon reached out towards evening we finally entered the long tree-lined drive that was the obligatory foreshadowing of all the new great houses. I was dropped half way along as the carrier was turning off to the estate farm. However, the trees gave some shelter from the storm and although I now had to lug my own bags along, at least water was no longer running down the back of my neck and spouting out through my sleeves as it had been for much of the day.

The sight of Stapleford Hall was all that I had hoped for. It was a large house built along the lines of the great houses, but more compact, modern and with warm buttery light blazing from all three floors. My welcome, if it could be called such, was not so inspiring.

"Euphemia St John! Hardly a name for a serving girl. Born on the wrong side of the blanket were you? I won't have any airs and graces on my staff."

The woman in front of me was tall, thin

and had a face like a half-starved crow; an effect compounded by the weight of sheer, and unusually shiny, dark hair wound tightly round her head. Her lips were a sliver of pink against a pale, angular face that was augmented by a pair of small black eyes. She was the very last person I would have chosen to help make my house a home. I dripped forlornly onto the unbeaten library carpet, tried not to be too distracted by the vast array of books, and hoped the fact I had begun to shiver from cold would go in my favour. I had already noticed the desk lamp badly needed polishing and this gave me hope.

"Well, girl, do you have a tongue in your head?"

"You could call me Amelia, Miss. It's my second name." I hadn't been foolish enough to change my Christian name. I was a girl without references and one who did not know her own name might shortly find herself being investigated by the local constabulary.

"Mrs Wilson. Mrs. All housekeepers and cooks are addressed as Mrs. You would know that if you'd ever been a maid before as your letter claimed."

"Yes, Mrs Wilson." I hung my head. "You are right."

The crow woman sniffed loudly. "You will find, should I chose to employ you, that I am always right. Though why I should employ a liar – give me one good reason."

"I do know the way things should be done, Mrs Wilson. I might not have been a maid before but . . ."

The door opened behind us admitting two gentlemen, who were in the process of arguing. "All I'm saying is the old geezer was my uncle too," complained a big thick-set man, with red hair and a voice thickened by the over-use of port.

"He was my godfather, Dickie," replied the shorter man. Both men were in evening dress, but my eye was quick to see that the second man, though arguably less handsome than the man-viking, had taken greater care over his tie and neatly oiled black locks.

"It's all very well, old boy," blustered the Viking, "but some of us have to damn well work for a living. All this health . . . hello, what's this, Mrs Wilson? Why is there a dab of a girl dripping on me Pater's carpet?"

I clenched my teeth, but kept my head down.

"I'm sorry to disturb you, Mr Richard. I was under the impression the family were all having cocktails. This girl was to have been the new maid."

"Was?" inquired the shorter man.

"It has become apparent she is not what she says she is. I doubt she has ever done a day's work in her life."

The shorter man approached me. "May I?" he asked and lifted my hands. He had a light touch and extraordinarily long and delicate fingers. He traced gently around the edge of my index fingers and across my palms. "A young woman used to writing, riding and light work would be my guess."

The Viking barked out a laugh. "Someone's discarded fancy-piece, Mrs Wilson. Won't do at all."

My head jerked up at the insult. The shorter man met my gaze and released my hands. "I don't believe so, Dickie."

"A by-blow then?"

"Do you find yourself without protection?" asked the man in front of me. His tone was cool and appraising, but I thought I detected sympathy in his eyes.

"My father died . . ." I stopped, suddenly overcome. I was cold. I was hungry. I had never felt more vulnerable. I wanted food. I wanted a bed and I wanted a big stick to beat the Viking for his insolence, but Mother and Little Joe were depending on me. I swallowed my pride. "There was no provision for me in his will."

"So who was this estimable father of yours,

young lady?" asked Dickie.

"I would prefer not to say, Sir."

"You're right, Mrs Wilson. Can't have a liar on the staff. Send the girl packing."

"As you wish Mr Richard."

"Wait," said the other man. "Look at me, girl. Is it a matter of honour that you cannot disclose your father's name?"

I met his gaze squarely, "Yes, Sir." My conscience pricked me, but I held my head up. The shorter man turned away to the others. "In which case, Mrs Wilson, I do not think it unreasonable that the girl be given a trial. It is not as if we are overflowing with servants at present."

Mrs Wilson bristled. "If you choose to be taken in, Mr Bertram, then there is nothing I can do. I'll present the case to the Mistress in the morning. If you would excuse us. Come girl." She opened a panel that I had taken to be real books and ushered me into a servants' passageway. "You might have fooled Mr Bertram, my girl, but you haven't fooled me," she hissed in my ear. "We'll see what the Mistress has to say about you. She's not one to be taken in."

She pushed me hard in the small of the back and I stumbled into darkness. The door closed behind us with a well oiled click. I stopped in my tracks as the light from the library vanished. Ahead of us a soft clamoring of metal upon metal could be heard. Mrs Wilson shoved me again down some stairs. "Get moving, girl. Any real servant would have known not to turn up minutes before dinner needs to be served."

I stumbled on not wishing to be trapped in the darkness any longer than was necessary with the harpy behind me. In only a few moments my eyes adjusted and I could see that as in the proverbial saying, there was light at the end of the tunnel. As we grew nearer to the exit the soft noises became harsher and interspersed with the barking cries of an angry woman.

We emerged directly into the kitchen. My initial impression was of thirty or more people burling around the room. I moved sharply aside before Mrs Wilson could shove me again and stepped on a large well polished shoe. "That," said Mrs Wilson coldly, "is Mr Holdsworth, the Butler."

"Sorry, Sir," I said timidly. A tall, stern faced middle-aged man with a polished demeanour looked down at me. His expression was cold, but I could see from the lines on his face he was normally no stranger to smiling. I bobbed a small curtsy and did my best to look friendly, but he said, "Don't let it happen again." His voice was strangely flat.

The room was modern and brightly lit. There was a fine range with sparkling pots. The high windows had been opened to combat the sweltering heat of a country house kitchen in full engine mode as the family were about to sit down to dinner.

"This is Mary," said the Butler indicating a pretty young woman with freckles and brown curls. "We call her Merry, because of her sunny disposition." I glanced up at him to see if he was joking, but his face gave no sign of levity. Merry on the other hand bounced over to shake my hand, a delighted smile on her face. "Help at last," she giggled. "It will be so nice to have another girl to work with. I can't really count Aggie, as all she ever talks about is how to get the pots cleaned faster."

"The scullery maid," explained Mr Holdsworth, "and this is the magnificent Mrs Deighton, who is coming to the end of the dinner preparations. It would probably be better if you were elsewhere while this process is completed. Perhaps Merry could show her to her room, Mrs Wilson? The girl needs to get out of those wet things." He then whispered to me, "We've had our tea, but I'm sure Mrs Deighton could find you a little something after dinner. She'll be much calmer then."

"We have not yet established whether Euphemia will be staying," snapped Mrs Wilson. "But you are quite correct, Mr Holdsworth. The girl is very wet. She dripped considerably on the library carpet. Merry, show her the way up to the library and give her some rags. I want that excess moisture mopped before the gentlemen retire for whisky. If you can do that right, girl, I might consider putting in a word for you with the Mistress."

I had the sense to nod and say, "Yes, Mrs Wilson. Thank you, Mrs Wilson." I'd rather have rammed her rags down her long rangy neck, but I suppressed the impulse and even managed a bobbed half-curtsy.

"You don't have to curtsy to me, girl," she snapped, but I could tell she was pleased. She had the same way about her as Bishop Pagget. I loathed her already.

Merry returned from a back room with a pile of rags, and with a wink and a nod gestured to me to follow her. "Mind you're not seen," called Mrs Wilson as we entered the passageway.

"Oh lor'," I muttered.

"Take no notice of her," said Merry. "She's a miserable, dry old stick, but half the time she's got her lips wrapped round a bottle and she don't bother us that much." She stopped by the library door. "Think you can find your way back?" I nodded in the gloom. "Right, I'll see you later then. Watch out for the gentlemen. You're so wet through it's like you're wearing no clothes." She giggled again and gave me a half pat, half shove through the door.

In the gas-light of the library I realised Merry was quite correct. My clothes were clinging far too closely to my form. No wonder the gentlemen had said what they did. I got down on my hands and knees, determined to get the job over with as quickly as possible.

My hands were numb with cold and I quickly discovered the rags had been previously used for polishing and had enough of the oils left on them to make them almost impervious to water. I pushed and dabbed at the carpet doing what I could, longing for the stifling warmth of the kitchen. Finally, I thought I had done the best possible under the circumstances. However, when I stood up I realised that where I had knelt I had left another wet patch. Cursing my own stupidity and Mrs Wilson's malevolence, I spread the driest of the rags on the floor at the edge of the new patch, knelt on that and applied myself to my impossible task. It was as much my fear I would be let go before being fed as my desire to prove myself that kept me going.

What seemed like a lifetime later, I stood up and looked down at the carpet. I had only succeeded in making it all worse. There was now even the odd smear of polish on the pale pattern. I could have screamed with frustration.

A door opened somewhere below and I realised the gentlemen must be on their way. Between facing them in my current state and facing Mrs Wilson I chose to retreat. I opened the passage entrance and darted through. In the darkness I tripped over something and landed flat on my face. My hands touched something wet.

Fortunately I was too numb from cold to feel any pain. My eyes were still adjusting to the gloom, but my fingers found a man's shoe. They travelled up to a trouser leg. "Excuse me," I whispered softly. But already I knew there was something solid and heavy about this form that was not right. I edged backward towards the door, my heart beating faster and faster. I pushed the panel and let the light from the library shine in through a crack. It took me several moments to understand what I was seeing.

The strip of pale yellow light fell upon a recumbent gentleman of middle age in evening dress. He was lying with his limbs tangled oddly about him. His gaze was fixed and distant. One hand was clutched to his chest and there was a pool of liquid spread around him. I pushed the door open wider and saw the full glory of his scarlet blood, the silver glint of the knife hilt and the death glaze on his pale blue eyes. Only then did I fully comprehend what I had found.

The Body in the Library

I briefly considered the option of swooning in a
ladylike manner, but I was denied this by virtue of
position: I was a maid; and by natural inclination:
I have never known how to swoon. Instead, I
did what I believe most females of sensibility
would have done finding themselves alone with a
murdered corpse. I screamed exceedingly loudly,
quite in the common manner, and pelted out of
the room.

I was, of course, still frozen to the bone,
so my egress was somewhat erratic. However,
I located the main door by reason of its size,
and skated, wet and panting to an awkward halt
with the balustrade of the upper landing wedged
firmly against my midriff. My screaming stopped
at once as all the air was punched out of me by

the ironwork.

Some fifteen feet below, the Butler, whose shoe I had recently trodden on, paused in his path towards the main door and stared up at me with the expression of a startled carp. A quite uncanny picture on a man, who though considerably older than I, was actually quite handsome.

When one has experienced a shocking happening, the most ridiculous things cross the mind.

The doorbell rang, loud and insistent, and doubtless not for the first time. Mr Holdsworth gave himself a small shake, tore his gaze away from me and continued his progress across the black and white tiled hall.

"Body," I gasped, leaning over the balcony. And then more loudly, "There's a body in the library."

I saw his shoulders stiffen, but the measured gait continued. Clearly, he was determined the presence of a mad woman in the house would not detain him from his duty of butler-ing.

Suddenly, I felt quite light-headed. My cold fingers found the balustrade and wrapped around it. The tiled floor swam beneath my eyes, and the elegant free-hung staircase that rose around the sides of the hall appeared to shiver, becoming a foaming river of marble. There was a particularly fine Persian rug in the middle of the hallway below. It clashed quite horribly with the tiles and before my bemused eyes the patterns began to pulse and swirl.

At that moment it seemed most likely one of two eventualities would occur. I would either shower the hall with the remnants of my breakfast or I would topple forward and decorate it with my brains. Either way I was about to make the most horrid mess, when I became dimly aware of the sound of running feet and a pair of strong arms pulled me back from the brink of disgrace and, or, death.

"Good gracious, Holdsworth," announced a female, with the voice of one educated at the most exclusive of seminaries, "is that wretched woman half drowning our maids now?"

I was led gently to a chair at the back of the balcony and when I demurred due to my wet raiment, was told quite forcibly to sit upon it.

"I believe," said Holdsworth, his voice to my ears coming from a long way away, "that the new maid has had a difficult journey through the recent storm. Mrs Wilson was most keen that she should clean up the library before supper." His tone remained respectful and yet still managed to convey his disapproval. Holdsworth was an excellent butler.

"Damn that woman!" said my female rescuer. Her language shocked me back to some sense of reality. I took note of her for the first time. A tall, red-headed woman with slightly too resolute a jaw to ever be a great beauty, but with the most fascinating green eyes. I could see little of her dress as she still wore a crimson cape, edged with fur, but I did see the most wonderful buttoned, brown boots that I guessed extended a goodly way over her slender ankles thus keeping out the winter chills. How I longed to be warm, but I too knew my duty.

"There's a body in the library, Miss." I felt I should apologise for the vulgarity of the announcement, but there was really no way but to say the thing.

As if in a bad play, Holdsworth and the young lady repeated my statement. It was clear I would have to explain further. "I was mopping the water from the rug in the library. I kept making it worse."

"I should think," commented the young lady.

I rudely continued. I had to say it all at once or it would never come out. "When I thought I heard someone coming, I thought to step into the servants' passage, but when I did I found the body of a man lying on the ground. He has a knife protruding from his chest."

Instead of cries of horror, two serious faces stared down at me. "It's true," I pleaded. "As God is my witness."

Holdsworth frowned and uttered that small cough servants make just before they are about to suggest that one's understanding of the situation is at fault. But before he could utter any words of butler-ish wisdom, the young lady cut him off. "Holdsworth, I think you'd better ring for the police."

"Surely Miss Richenda, you cannot believe this young woman is correct? She is feverish with cold and hunger."

"Possibly. But her eyes look clear. I've seen a lot of fever and hunger in the shelters, and she looks more shocked to me. Not that meeting Mrs Wilson wouldn't be a shock to anyone's system." Miss Richenda uttered an unladylike bark of laughter. It was so inappropriate to the circumstances that I felt tears sting my eyes.

"I am sure it will prove to be nothing, Miss," soothed Holdsworth.

"Let's find out," said Miss Richenda. "C'mon girl, show us where your body is."

To my surprise I found my legs were able to function. I tottered ahead. The library was as I had left it with the door to the servants' passage still open. By the light of the lamps I could make out the shadow of a man's leg. I turned my face away and pointed. Miss Richenda dived forward into the passage.

"Good Lord above, the girl is right, Holdsworth. Come and have a look."

"Thank you, Miss. I will take your word for it if you don't mind. I shall now go to summon the police and inform the household."

"Right-o," said Richenda. "Couldn't bring me a lamp, could you, girl?"

"Me, Miss?"

"Oh blow that! Give me a hand and we'll have him out into the light."

I had always known a servant's lot was not a happy one, as surely as I knew if I did not obey Miss Richenda I would be back out in the rain looking for a new position. Reminding myself that I had my mother's spirit (and that of all her ancestors) within me, I closed my eyes, stepped forward and grabbed a leg.

Dead bodies are remarkably heavy. It is as if when life departs, a heavier matter takes the empty seat of the soul. It took us time, with unbecoming comments from the lady and a fair bit of grunting on my part, but we dragged the man into the light of the library.

It was unfortunate that at this moment Merry rushed into the room, took one look at our hard won corpse and burst into tears.

"My goodness," cried Miss Richenda. "It's Cousin Georgie!"

Merry wailed.

I don't think I had ever heard someone actually wail before; Father had always kept me away from the graveside during funerals. It is a high pitched keening that I would not care to hear again. Miss Richenda did not care for the noise either. She stomped over to Merry and gave her a smart slap across the face. The noise abated immediately. Merry cowered, her eyes huge and haunted.

"What on earth is the matter with you, girl? He's my cousin, not yours."

"I think, Miss, some deal better with death than others," I said, crossing to the quivering Merry and putting one damp arm around her thin shoulders. "We're not all made of such stern stuff as yourself."

"Humph! Didn't hear you screeching like a banshee." She paused. I kept quiet, fearing I had already overstepped the mark. "What yer doing here anyway, Merry?"

"I was sent by Mr Holdsworth to provide comfort," Merry whispered.

I failed to wipe the sudden smile from my face this comment inspired before Miss Richenda noticed. But rather than lambasting me, she grinned broadly. "Comfort! Ha!"

"Also," continued Merry timidly, "the Mistress would like to see Euphemia."

"Oh Lor' if dearest Step-Mama wants you

girl, you'd better hop to it. My father's latest wife might speak softly, but she's a bigger harridan than the Wilson monstrosity."

I was in equal parts taken aback by her comment and grateful for the warning. I bobbed a curtsy and looked hopefully at Merry. "I'll need to take her, Miss. Her being new. Will you be all right alone with . . . him?" Her voice wavered piteously on the last word.

Richenda shooed us away. "I'm made of stern stuff. I'll stand guard. Send that wimp Holdsworth along. There should be two of us here."

Merry and I bobbed obediently. Feeling had returned to my limbs, and my ankles and knees were beginning to hurt abominably with all this wretched dipping. Being a maid was turning out to be far worse than I had expected and I hadn't even been engaged yet.

"She'll see you in the green drawing-room," Merry threw over a shoulder as she scurried along the hallway. "C'mon we mustn't be seen."

"Shouldn't we be using the servants' passage?" I asked lumbering after her as fast as my damp skirts would allow. Merry might be a slender, little thing, but she fairly flew along when she set her mind to it.

"Not bloody likely! Who's to say the murderer isn't still in there?"

"If he is," I reasoned, "he could pop out in

any room that had an entrance. So we wouldn't be safe anywhere."

Merry stopped. I caught my breath. "You are a one for imaginings, aren't you? That won't go down well with the Mistress."

"I shall be nothing but polite and servile with Her Ladyship," I assured her.

Merry considered me with her head on one side. "I'm not sure you know how," she said after a moment's thought. "There's something different about you. Can't quite put me finger on it."

"You were very upset earlier. You all right now?" I deflected.

"It was the shock."

"Of course," I said affably, "only I got the impression it was something more. Something I can't quite put my finger on yet."

"The green drawing-room is this way."

Merry took off again, and after a dizzying number of twists and turns, we stopped outside two large, pale double doors. My best guess was that we were now in the East Wing, but I couldn't be sure.

"It's in here," said Merry. "Don't knock. She hates knocking. Says it gets on her nerves."

"I can't just barge in. I might disturb her. See something I shouldn't. It's rude."

"What are you thinking of?" asked Merry, her hands on her hips. "We're servants. The likes of them don't give a hoot for what we see. We don't matter except when they want food or hot water or something moved. We don't count."

I'd made a bad mistake, but I caught the note of bitterness behind her words. "I'm sorry," I said quickly, "the lady who trained me liked us to knock."

"I thought you said you hadn't been in service before?"

"Did I? It wasn't proper service. She was training me as a favour."

Thankfully, Merry didn't ask who the favour was to. Instead she sucked at her teeth, and then as if suddenly making up her mind, she nodded. "There's something rum about you, me girl, but I won't forget you was kind to me when I was upset."

The green drawing-room, much like its central figure, was somewhat faded. Lady Stapleford awaited me in a large winged chair facing out from the central fireplace. The hearth was filled with dried flowers. Accordingly the room was very cold. The ambiance was further depressed by the sound of rain lashing against the windowpanes.

My initial impression of the Mistress of the house was one of a slight lady encased in many layers of cloth. My eyes wandered to her face for a moment and met such a look of shocked reproof, that I kept them slightly lowered as I approached.

However, I could see something of the room as I walked towards her. The curtains were closed and the room was lit by gas lamps around the walls that cast flickering shadows. There was furniture everywhere. Seating of various sorts was placed around the room in what some might have called fashionable disarray, and others a mess. Beside the lady was an occasional table on which stood an untidy clutter of things, and around the room were several more little tables with ornaments, china and glass upon them. I picked my way carefully through until I was finally in front of the chair. I felt, as I was surely meant to, that I was being given an audience with someone extremely important. Or at least someone who thought themselves important.

"So, you are the young woman who discovered a dead man in my library. Outrageous!"

Lady Stapleford's English was almost perfect. There was a trace of a French accent, but it was more a softening of the edges of the cut-glass speech of the Stapleford children. Richenda had referred to Lady Stapleford as her father's latest wife, a criticism that was either totally unfounded or Lord Stapleford had a penchant for ageing blondes on the dark side of forty.

Everything about Lady Stapleford was soft,

from her downy hair to her flowing layers of ribbons and lace. She must have once been very, very beautiful, but now the twin flames of beauty and youth had deserted her. In her sharp blue eyes I saw the shadows of despair at the cruelty of ageing. Unlike Mother, who had never had much beauty to lose, Lady Stapleford was unwisely clinging to fashion and French scent.

"Yes, Ma'am," I answered, hoping that she was referring to the body as outrageous rather than my discovery.

"We have never had anything like it in all my time as Mistress of Stapleford Hall."

"I'm sure, it's most distressing, My Lady."

"What were you doing in the library anyway, girl?"

"I was mopping the carpet, My Lady."

"Mopping? Had there been a flood?" The cold sapphire eyes swept up and down my form.

"It was raining when I arrived, My Lady."

"And you decided to dry yourself by rolling on my Persian library carpet?"

Now, that carpet was as Persian as our family pig, but I didn't think it would help my case to point this out.

"No, My Lady. It is where Mrs Wilson was good enough to interview me."

Another cold, hard stare.

"I dripped."

"You dripped?" Lady Stapleford couldn't have sounded more scandalised if I'd confessed to stealing the silver.

"I'm very sorry, My Lady. The storm was in full force when I was walking up the drive."

"Walking up the drive? Were you just passing and took it into your head to visit my housekeeper?"

"Of course not, My Lady. I was engaged by letter."

"What's your name?"

"Euphemia St John, Ma'am."

"That is a totally unsuitable name for a servant. I would advise you to change it at once if you wish to gain employment."

Oh dear, this wasn't sounding good. I attempted my most contrite expression. "I was hoping to be in service here, My Lady."

"I do comprehend that, young woman, but not only do you have the most ridiculous – one might even suggest false – name, you discovered a body in my library."

"It was in the servants' passage, Ma'am," I muttered.

"Nonsense! My step-nephew would never have entered the servants' quarters." She flushed pink. "I have it on Holdsworth's authority that the body is lying on my Persian carpet."

"But it's not . . ."

"Do you dare contradict me?"

Talking to Lady Stapleford was like playing some bizarre game of chess, where at her whim all the pieces exchanged moves. I completely understood she was angry, upset, perhaps even a little afraid about the death of her relative and that she wanted someone to blame. It was unfortunate I was the nearest person. Not only my pride, but an extremely long walk home, was at stake in this conversation.

I bobbed a curtsy. "Of course you're right, Ma'am. The murderer must have put the body in the passage."

"Murderer?"

"Miss Richenda and I pulled the body into the library."

Lady Stapleford leant back in her chair looking quite faint. From somewhere beneath her gown she produced an old fashioned fan and waved if feebly. With one trembling hand she pointed to the decanter of water on the occasional table beside her. I took the hint, poured her a glass and handed it over with another curtsy. Her long, red fingernails grazed the side of my index finger as she grasped the glass. With great effort she took a couple of sips before flinging the glass back at me. I had some idea of what might be coming and innocently intercepted it before I became any wetter. (If such a thing was possible.)

"Am I to understand," said Lady Stapleford in a breathless voice, "that you persuaded my step-daughter to aid you in moving the body? That between you you picked up my dead step-nephew and carried him into the library?"

"We . . . er . . . pulled him, My Lady." If only my father had not taught me to be truthful.

"Pulled?"

"We took a leg each."

Out came the fan once more. I quickly filled up the glass.

"Really,"said Lady Stapleford when she had finished waving and gulping down a whole glass. "The girl is quite unmanageable."

I saw a glimmer of hope. She was talking about Richenda. I kept my mouth shut and hoped.

"You need not think I hold you excused, young woman. However, I will not have anyone say I am an unreasonable woman."

"I'm sure no one would dream of it, My Lady."

Her Ladyship continued as if she had not heard me. "In the spirit of Christian charity, you will be allowed to take a little supper of leftovers before leaving."

"Leaving?" I gasped. "At this time of night? In this storm?"

"Pah! A little rain never hurt anyone."

"A little rain?" I said faintly. I was about to enlighten Lady Stapleford on my view's of her Christian charity when the door behind me opened.

"A policeman, Your Ladyship," announced Holdsworth.

A small stout man in a greenish bowler hat and worn, shiny suit entered. He matched some of the furnishing. "Good evening to you, My Lady. I was enquiring as to the whereabouts of the young lady who found the body and was told she was with you."

Lady Stapleford inclined her head towards me. "I was about to dismiss her."

"Oh, I couldn't recommend that, My Lady. Look most odd like. If you forgive me saying so. Besides, the Inspector will want a word. Best to keep the girl on the premises until this is all over. Bird in the bush, if you catch my drift."

Lady Stapleford gave me a look of pure loathing, but at least the prospect of a long walk home had receded from my immediate future. I gave the policeman my sunniest smile.

A Policeman's Lot

"If you don't mind my saying so, Miss, you look a trifle on the damp side," pronounced the grey-haired Sergeant Davies as he poured me a second cup of tea. "It's not regular to be giving witnesses tea, but I reckon how the Inspector would like it if you expired from pneumonia before he had the chance to interview you himself."

We were sitting in Mrs Deighton's lovely, modern, bright and wonderfully warm kitchen. The Sergeant had insisted I put my chair near the range. It was a hard wooden seat, but I had never felt more comfortable or more blissful as I sipped my hot tea and admired, through the windows behind Sergeant Davies, the pattern of stars glittering in the night sky. Even Lady Stapleford would surely balk at turning me out into the darkness – what with her reputation of being a Christian soul to uphold.

"There now, if she isn't getting the colour back into her cheeks," said the redoubtable Mrs Deighton, who had opted to stay alert and maintain a flow of tea and edible support for the staff and family in this crisis.

Tears stung my eyes. That two people who didn't know me from Eve and who didn't have a good reason for ruling me out as a murderer, or at least a suspicious person, were being so kind.

"There, there, pet. Don't you go upsetting yourself. She's had a most difficult day, Officer. What she needs is her bed."

Sergeant Davies produced a small notebook. He flicked open the top with a practised air, retrieved a pencil from behind his ear and licked it once. He hovered his pencil above the fresh page. "It was my understanding that the young lady has not yet been engaged. In which case she won't necessarily be having a bed to be sleeping in." He paused significantly. "If this be the case then I expect I shall have to be taking her back to the station house with me to sleep in a cell." I gasped. "Sorry, Miss, but I can't let you go tramping around the countryside at this time of night."

"But I don't want to be locked up," I whined miserably and idiotically, adding the most suspicious of phrases, "I haven't done anything."

"That might be the case, but there's a law against vagrants around here and if I was to be letting you loose into the night I'd only have to follow you and pick you up later. Far better for me to take you down as a guest than have to arrest you later. I'll do my best to get you a single cell."

Out of the corner of my eye I caught sight of Mrs Wilson lurking in the shadows of the doorway. A shaft of starlight showed me the approving sneer on her face. I think the Sergeant saw too, because he added, " 'Course, it's a shame and all. Ain't going to do the Staplefords' reputation any good that I've got to go hauling servants from their house down to the jail. I know you says how she's not been engaged yet, but you know how folks natter and the stories wot they tell often bears no resemblance to the honest truth."

Mrs Deighton put her hand to her cheek. "Oh, Sergeant Davies, you don't say! Likely the Mistress will have someone's hide for a tale like that starting."

I felt it was a bit overdone, but Mrs Wilson caved. "Of course Euphemia is engaged. I've only this moment been satisfying myself that her room is ready."

I smiled too loudly, for the harpy added, "The engagement is naturally on a trial basis. A two week trial."

I remembered to be meek this time, bowing my head, and murmuring, "Yes, Mrs Wilson. Of course, Mrs Wilson. I will endeavour to the utmost of my ability to give complete satisfaction, Mrs Wilson."

"Merry will show you up when the policeman is done with you. If you would like to follow me, Sergeant, I have found a quiet room, as you asked, for statements to be taken."

"Right then, Euphemia," said Sergeant Davies, "you're first. Seeing as you found the body."

The room she showed us into was to my surprise above stairs, but then I suppose she had recalled that people of all rank would be interviewed. It was a small square box off the hallway with a single window looking out onto the drive. There was a small desk, a table, three wooden chairs and a single coat-stand in it. The small ironwork hearth was scrubbed, but empty. It was very cold.

"I trust this will suit your needs, Sergeant?" said Mrs Wilson, clearly not expecting a response.

"Perfect. Perfect, Mrs Wilson. I reckon you've done a fine job getting all them coats and wellies cleared out and the furniture brought up."

Mrs Wilson had the grace to blush. "I am not

accustomed to having the police in the house."

"I'm glad to hear it Ma'am. Now if you could just be doing with lighting the fire. Ain't no saying when the man from The Yard might be turning up. Scotland Yard that is, Ma'am. One of our top men."

"I will send someone to see to it," said Mrs Wilson in a voice that I swear iced up the window.

As Mrs Wilson swept out I looked at Sergeant Davies with renewed approval.

"Now, there ain't no use grinning at me, Miss. You sit yourself down and take things serious while I work out what I've done with my notebook. Ah-ha." He produced the wanted article from his trouser pocket. It was now somewhat dog-eared. Sergeant Davies frowned hard at it, but the edges did not uncurl themselves and he was reduced to bending them back into shape with his fingers. While he was doing this, the scullery maid appeared with a coal scuttle and kindling. Soon the fire was roaring nicely.

Sergeant Davies asked me to start at the beginning. He listened with little comment, except for the occasional nod of encouragement or grunt of acknowledgment. I was a little awkward at first, but after a hesitant start the words quickly began to flow. To my surprise, I found telling my tale, especially to such a sympathetic audience, lightened a load on my chest I had not been aware I was carrying. Sergeant Davies' eyebrows rose somewhat when I described how Mrs Wilson had sent me to mop up the library. "That's why I'm so wet," I explained and he merely nodded, but I saw a kindly understanding in his eyes.

Like most, I have had my experiences with the less than fast thinking country policeman, but while I had no reason to think Sergeant Davies a genius, he appeared to be listening hard and making many notes. I had just got to the part of my tale where Miss Richenda and I grabbed a leg each when he suddenly stopped writing and held up his hand.

"You moved the body?"

"Well, yes. I did say I found it in the corridor."

"So it didn't tumble out when you opened the door?"

"No."

"You're certain about that Miss?"

"Absolutely. It took the two of us a lot of effort to drag him out. I'm stronger than I look and Miss Richenda is rather large."

Sergeant Davies closed his eyes as if in pain and rubbed the bridge of his nose. "So I am to understand that you two, young ladies, you two strong young ladies, had no qualms about grabbing the legs of a corpse and dragging it some ten feet across the floor?"

"It was more like twenty."

"Whose idea was it to move the body?"

"I'm not sure," I thought back. "I think it was Miss Richenda's. She wanted to have a good look at him in the light. I thought it was a good idea."

"You thought it was a good idea?" repeated the Sergeant in astonished accents. Then Davies slammed his open palm down on the table. "Did you never hear how important it is not to disturb a body at a murder scene?!"

I quailed slightly at this sudden change in temperament, but answered, I felt very reasonably, "I do not have much experience with dead bodies, Sir."

"Much experience?" picked up the far too intelligent Sergeant. "How many dead bodies have you discovered, young woman?"

"Only two," I answered, again cursing my upbringing for schooling me to always be truthful. I fancied I could see deep suspicion behind the policeman's eyes.

"And 'ho, exactly, was this other one?"

"The Reverend Joshia Martins of Sweetfield Parish. He died of very natural causes. In his mutton and onions." A part of me was willing my mouth to quieten, but my tongue kept skipping along. "There were absolutely no suspicious circumstances. You can check."

"That I will. And you were maid to this Reverend Martins? Cook-maid?"

Oh Lord forgive me, there it was . . . If I answered this truthfully, I would be not only exposed as a fraud, but probably also made a strong contender for the role of murderer. After all, I'd wormed my way into the house on the flimsiest of pretexts and the murder had been committed within moments of my arrival. Even I felt I was a suspicious character.

"I lived in, but I had no cooking duties," I said, praying silently for my eternal soul, as I uttered this half-truth. It was true we had had a maid and it was true she'd found my father dead at the table. With the vicarage dispersed I could only hope that the Sergeant would not enquire too closely, or that the murderer would quickly be found.

At that moment I made up my mind to help him as much as I could. It wasn't only that I felt some absurd responsibility towards the dead man for finding him – although I did, and I felt quite terrible about dragging his corpse around by the leg now I had had time to think about it – but it was going to be in my very best interests for the murderer to be uncovered quickly before anyone started delving too closely into my background.

Without warning, the front door crashed open and we heard the sharp footsteps of someone storming across the hall. "Holdsworth! Wilson! Fetch the Mistress. I want an explanation of what is going on in my house!"

The Sergeant folded up his notebook and put it away. "We will speak again, Miss." He nodded at the door, and taking my cue I crept out into the hall. Mindful of the rule of not being seen by the family, I stepped behind a very large plant that had grown to a considerable height above its shiny brass container. From this position I was able to observe the master of the house as he yelled for all and everyone to attend him.

Sir Stapleford was, I guessed, in his early sixties, but still in excellent health if his energetic striding was anything to go by. As he paced, far too close to my hiding place for comfort, I was able to ascertain he was not a tall man, being around my height, and that he smelled of cigars and cologne. He was stout with the fleshy face of one who has enjoyed during his lifetime a surfeit of fresh meat and fine wine. His nose was growing increasingly claret red with each bellow. He reminded me a great deal of Farmer Forbes' oxen when he was late with their feed.

Unlike the glorious brown mantle of those creatures, Lord Stapleford's thinning hair was dark and plastered slick to his head with some fashionable product. His eyes were small and retracted, practically buried above the copious jowls of his face. His neck hung over the side of his collar in a most unattractive manner, but his clothing and shoes were of the best quality.

Holdsworth arrived first. His progression across the tiles was quick, but no one could have accused him of scurrying; it was more of a glide. He carried before him a small silver tray on which was perched a large glass of whisky. He came into dock before Sir Stapleford, who took the glass without thinking, downed the contents and continued to berate all those within earshot. "Some damn fool rung up my office and said there'd been a murder here."

"That would have been I, Sir," said Holdsworth bowing impressively without dropping tray or glass. "I fear . . ."

We were never to learn what the Butler feared as at that moment Richenda appeared at the top of the stairs.

"Dear Papa," she cried, trotting down the stairs – I would have liked to have used the more feminine word tripping, but in all honesty I cannot – "I have come home. And I have found a body. Isn't it all just ripping?"

"Ripping! Ripping!" bellowed her father. "Did I send you to Switzerland to hear, to see, you conduct yourself with such unbecoming, unbecoming, unbecoming . . ."

"Conduct?" suggested Richenda, reaching

the bottom of the stairs and coming over to give her father a kiss on the cheek.

"Does this mean you've given up that damn fool business?"

"Now, Father what can you mean?"

"That London tomfoolery."

"It's hardly tomfoolery, Father. We are having questions asked in the House."

"Good God, girl! Do you want to die a spinster? I strongly doubt any man would take you in hand even if I paid him."

Richenda flushed scarlet. "That's a terrible thing to say."

"Still holding out hopes of a marriage then, daughter? Home to use my money as bait on some poor fish you've got nibbling in your pool, are you? Because I'm telling you now, girl, it won't wash. You'll get nothing out of me while you persist in making a spectacle of yourself. Nothing. Won't even have you in my house. That's what I said and damn it that's what I mean."

"As you wish, Papa. I hope you remember when you are old, grey, senile and alone that it was you who sent me away."

"If I'm senile I doubt I'll remember anything, what!" barked Sir Stapleford. "Silly girl. Don't try and keep up with the men, Richenda, you've not got the brains for it."

"I hate you," spat his daughter. "I wish you

were dead."

Sir Stapleford turned his back on his daughter, "That reminds me, Holdsworth, what is all this body business about?"

"If I might presume, Sir," said Sergeant Davies, who had been calmly observing the scene from the sidelines, "I'm Sergeant Davies, sent up by the local station while we're waiting for one of our top men to arrive from The Yard."

"Top man from The Yard?" echoed Sir Stapleford blankly.

"I regret to inform you, Sir, that your nephew the Honourable George Pierre Lafayette has been found murdered on your premises," he referred to his notebook, "by a young maid, Euphemia St John, shortly after the family had sat down to dinner."

"Nonsense. Nonsense," snapped Sir Stapleford, "we don't have a maid of that name. Besides, only a nephew by marriage. My first wife's sister's child. Saw him at the club a few days ago. In perfect health."

"Well, he's not in good health no more, Sir."

I was distracted from hearing Sir Stapleford's answer by a sharp pain in my right ear. "Time, I think, for listening ears to go to their bed," hissed Mrs Wilson in my ear. She nodded politely to the assembled company and pulled me from my hiding place by the ear. Several pairs of astonished eyes followed my embarrassing and painful progress as Mrs Wilson dragged me to the back of the hall, through a door and onto the servants' staircase. If I had had any idea that she might let go when there were no longer witnesses to shame me I was quite wrong. By the time we reached the attic my ear was raw and throbbing.

Mrs Wilson opened what I took to be a cupboard door and thrust me through. "You'll be awakened at dawn for chores before breakfast." She closed the door behind me.

The cupboard was dark, but it had a window and as my eyes grew accustomed to the moonlight I realised this was my room. I quickly discovered the ceiling was not of uniform height by the unfortunate method of testing it with my head. I sat down heavily on the single bed and marvelled how such a modern house, with every obvious modern convenience, had yet made no more provision for its servants than these small coombed attic rooms. However, I had had a long, shocking, adventurous and if I am as honest as usual, quite terrifying day. I slipped out of my outer dress and climbed under the all too thin covers. My mother would have been appalled, but even if Mrs Wilson had had the kindness to send up my things to the room, I was not going to hunt for them in the darkness and risk a further, and potentially more serious, concussion.

My poor bed was beginning to feed back some little warmth into my bones, when I became aware of the sound of sobbing. It says something for my tiredness of mind that it first occurred to me that Mrs Wilson was harpy enough to give me the one haunted room in the house. "Quiet, please," I murmured. "You're wasting your time. I don't believe in ghosts." I shoved my head under the covers, emerging a moment later to add, "And my father was a vicar, so I know."

The sobbing continued unabated.

Sighing, I sat up carefully and tried to guess its direction. As far as I could tell, it was coming from somewhere to the right of my room. I got up, wrapping a cover around me for warmth as much as decency, and opened my door. I needn't have worried about propriety; it was pitch black in the corridor. I felt my way along. I was sleepy enough not to consider the wisdom of my action fully and opened the first door I came across, trusting there would be no men on this side of the attic. It was a linen closet. I discovered this by walking into some shelves and having their contents fall down on my head. After this I was more cautious. I listened at the next door and thought I heard the faint sound of sobbing. I knocked softly. "Is there anyone there?" I enquired, feeling like a second rate medium.

"Is that you, Euphemia?" came Merry's voice

from within. "Wait a minute."

There was the sound of footsteps and then a bolt being drawn back. The door opened, and standing with a lit candlestick in her hand was a tear-stained Merry. "You lost?" she asked.

"No, I'm next door."

Merry attempted to wipe away the tears with the back of her free hand. "I'm sorry. It's been a right bad day."

"You could say that."

"I did," replied Merry, puzzled.

"Why are you crying?"

"The murder and everything."

"It's more than that, isn't it?"

Merry, probably realising I was not going to go away, grabbed me by the arm and pulled me into her room. Her fingernails nipped. These people certainly had a nasty habit of hauling each other around by body parts. Or perhaps it was fate somehow paying me back for what I had done to Georgie and his leg.

"Get in here. We'll both lose our places if the Wilson catches us."

Merry's room was not unlike I imagined my own dark little cupboard to be. It was cheerier, but then the candlelight helped a lot. I could see a couple of postcards tucked under her washstand. On one I could see a bit of the Eiffel Tower. Merry caught the direction of my gaze and backed into the stand, pushing the postcards under with the tips of her fingers. Suddenly, I thought I understood. "You were fond of George Lafayette, weren't you?"

Merry looked at me defiantly for a moment. Then bit her lip and nodded, bowing her head. She was a very pretty girl with the right amount of spark to appeal to a young man about town. Inwardly I rained down curses on the dead man's head.

"Are you in trouble, Merry?"

Her chin flew up. "Of course I'm not. What do you take me for? I'm not that kind of a girl. Me and Mr Georgie were friends like."

My disbelief must have shown on my face.

"And why not? You're as bad as Mr Holdsworth! Miss Richenda's got her odd beliefs. Mr Georgie said he personally 'ad no difficulty with my station. He said I was smart as a whip and twice as pretty as any society girl he'd ever known. What's wrong with that?"

It crossed my mind that though Merry was obviously country-born she might not have had the advantage of being brought up alongside farms and thus be as familiar as I with the more detestable urges of the male animal. She honestly might not know what was wrong with that. "What did you and Mr Georgie do?"

"We talked. He was fascinated by what we

did below stairs. He said how I was taken for granted."

"What else?"

"Nothing."

"Merry?"

"Nothing! I swear."

Now, I knew she was lying.

"Merry?"

"Oh, alright, he kissed me once. But he apologised at once. Said he was right ashamed of himself, but that I was so sweet he couldn't help himself. He said he thought of me like a little sister."

"He kisses his sister?" I asked, shocked.

"No, he doesn't have a sister. He meant I was like a sister to him. He sent me postcards from the world. Places he said he would have shown me if things were different. He said there was always hope and that maybe if we could prove our attachment was strong enough people would forget I was a servant."

"And how, exactly, were you to prove this?"

"I don't know. He died before he could tell me," Merry began to wail. I managed to take the candlestick from her before she tumbled onto the bed and gave herself up to despair. I knew it would be a long time before she could understand that fate had saved her from a most grim future. Rather than point this out, I petted her and stroked her arm, and talked a lot of nonsense about how he must have died at once without pain and how if he cared for her he wouldn't want her to be unhappy. Finally, she stopped sobbing and slipped into slumber.

As it would have been dangerous to leave the sleeping Merry with a lit candle, I took it with me. It would make finding my door much easier and would hopefully prevent any more bruises before I too could collapse into sleep.

By now I was dropping with exhaustion. I opened my door thinking of nothing but my bed. A chilly blast blew out my candle, but not before I saw that my room had been thoroughly ransacked.

Behind the Scenes

"Did you not think to alert the rest of the household, Euphemia?"

"I thought there was little point," I said quietly. I was discovering how very imposing a large man in an immaculate butler suit could be. This was a very different Mr Holdsworth from the one who had let me step on his foot.

"It seems to me, Miss St John," said the Butler, bringing into play a manly but sarcastic eyebrow raise that under different circumstances I might have found attractive, "that you did not engage your brain at all. Merry, I might forgive such foolishness, but you are cut from a different cloth."

The back handed compliment felt like a slap in the face.

"Yes, Mr Holdsworth."

Moments later I was literally upon the carpet in the library repeating my explanation to Sergeant Davies, who was in the process of inspecting the site where Richenda and I had dragged the body. A screen that had been placed around the bloodied site now stood forlornly off to one side of the large fireplace.

The Sergeant was not in a good humour and was equally unimpressed by my silence. "Did you not think, Miss, that the intruder might still have been in the house?"

"We might all have been murdered in our beds," explained Mrs Wilson, who I believe had invited herself to this interview under the guise of being my chaperone. Whereas in reality, I could see in her needle sharp eyes the keenest of desires to find any reason to remove me from my position.

"I think that is unlikely, Mrs Wilson," responded Mr Holdsworth. "It is more likely that the family would have been relieved of their silver."

I gave him a grateful smile.

"Which would have been a most serious matter," added the Butler frowning upon me. I schooled my expression to a suitable contrition.

"Perhaps she was in league with the burglar!" cried Mrs Wilson. "Why else would she not report the intrusion?"

All eyes turned to me. Mr Bertram rose from a wing-backed chair which had previously concealed his presence and said, "That is a most serious charge, Mrs Wilson."

"I hate to admit," said Sergeant Davies, "but the head maid has a point."

"Housekeeper," hissed Mrs Wilson.

"You had better explain yourself, Miss," the policeman continued.

I had been prepared to defend the lie I was concealing, but to be accused of something of which I was totally innocent threw me onto my back foot. (An expression my father used and which I believe refers to pugilism. Although crude, it is not entirely inappropriate for my situation, as I was about to be fighting for my life and situation, though fortunately with words rather than blows. Little Joe informs me I am not capable of forming a passable fist.) I am ashamed to say I took refuge in the weakness of my sex and covered my face with my hands. I know nothing of play-acting, again contrary to popular vaudeville songs it is not the sort of thing vicars' daughters are encouraged to pursue, but I think I achieved a few credible sobs.

"How can you think such a thing, Mrs Wilson?" I sobbed. "It was on receipt of your letter that I left my last situation to come and work with you! Without this I have nothing and my family are depending on me."

"Is it true, Mrs Wilson?" asked Sergeant Davies. "Did you write to this young woman to appoint her?"

"Well, yes," said my nemesis, "but only in reply to her letter. She responded to an advertisement we placed in the paper. She could have planned this from the very start. I always said she was no proper maid. I suspect in both senses if you take my meaning."

My head snapped up at the insult. Did the woman's spite know no bounds? "Of course, it makes a great deal of sense that once my accomplice has murdered his victim I should stay on working at the house! Has it not occurred to any of you that this may be the way the assailant left? That it was a break-out rather than a break-in. That the intruder fled across the rooftops?"

I did indeed think it was possible the intruder had remained in the house, but I was concealing the timing of events. My conscience reproached me, but I knew I must keep things simple and divert suspicion away from myself. I also knew I was guilty of no terrible misdemeanor.

Mr Bertram strolled over to lean against the fireplace. It was the action of a man seeking warmth from the fire, but I was left with the peculiar sensation that he repositioned himself the better to regard myself. I confess there was a part of me that hoped this was the case. "You must admit that is a more interesting idea, Sergeant," he said. His dark eyes surveyed me unblinkingly, but at least, unlike the Sergeant, he wasn't scowling at me.

"So you are saying, Miss, these ideas occurred to you last night, and yet you didn't think to tell anyone?"

"Yes. I mean no," I stammered unsure of the morality of revealing Merry's confession that had so distracted me. I compromised. "The maid near me, Merry, was most distressed by the events yesterday in the house. I went to her to ask for assistance and ended up comforting her tears."

"Rubbish," snapped Mrs Wilson. "Why should Merry be distressed? The foolish nickname the staff have given should be proof of her temperament. I say the girl was in league with a burglary that went wrong and ended in the death of poor Mr George."

"I would expect any of the staff to be distressed by the appalling events in the house," said Mr Bertram quietly, but firmly. "Moreover, Merry has been with us a long time and would naturally be disturbed by any death in the family. To say nothing of such a violent ending to poor Cousin George's existence."

"Of course, Sir. Any of the mature members

of staff, but these silly girls . . ."

Sergeant Davies cut her off. "Thank you, Mrs Wilson. If I might carry on with my examination. Now, Miss, what gave you the idea the intruder and the murderer were the same?"

"It seems somewhat beyond coincidence, Sergeant, that the family, important though the Staplefords doubtless are, should be targeted by two villains on the same day. It is not as if the house is in the heart of the metropolis."

Mr Bertram made an odd sound and covered his mouth with his hand. I thought I saw his moustache twitch.

"Also when I and Miss Richenda discovered the body . . ."

"Miss Richenda and I," hissed a scandalised Mrs Wilson.

I gave her a token nod. "When Miss Richenda and I discovered the body . . ."

"I thought you discovered the body alone, Miss."

"Well, yes, that's true, but I ran immediately from the room. It was Miss Richenda who persuaded me to return with her so we could identify the body."

"She will be blaming Miss Richenda next. You mark my words. The girl is a born liar," whispered Mrs Wilson to Mr Bertram. I was glad to see he turned his shoulders away from the poisonous crow of a woman. I attempted to ignore her.

"So while I did find the body, it is more accurate to say I discovered it with Miss Richenda. When I fled from the passage I was quite overset and to be frank not at all sure what I had encountered. I had been travelling through a storm for the best part of the day. I was cold and tired and had had nothing to eat since breakfast. I think at the moment I ran I was hoping it was no more than a conjuring of my overwrought nerves. I am very sorry to be wrong."

"Why did you go to the library, Miss?"

"Mrs Wilson sent me. I had initially been interviewed by her earlier that evening in the library. After we left, she remarked on the water damage I had left on the carpet and asked me to return to repair it."

Sergeant Davies scribbled in his notebook. "I see, Miss. And was Mrs Wilson out of your sight between your first encountering her and your return to the library?"

I hesitated. "It was all very confusing when I arrived and I was very tired and hungry. There was a great deal for me to take notice upon," I began maliciously. I had the gratification of seeing Mrs Wilson pale and begin to stammer incoherently. The Sergeant held up his hand to her and I continued, "But no, Sergeant. I believe

I was constantly in the presence of Mrs Wilson until I was sent to the library. At that point she remained behind in the kitchen . . ."

"I had the family's dinner to attend to," protested the annoying woman.

"She certainly did not enter the library again before I encountered the body in the servants' passageway." I let my tone strengthen a little on the last two words and again had the gratification of seeing Mrs Wilson pale. I think it was at this point that I did genuinely begin to wonder if the woman had anything to do with the murder. A housekeeper is a constant presence in the house, sharing not only many of the family's secrets, but also being closer to them than most of the staff. I believe in some families there is often a bond between the master of the house and butler, but really having servants is almost as unenvious a business as being one.

The Sergeant watched me closely. He swung round suddenly to Mrs Wilson. "Would you say, Mrs Wilson, that this is a happy house?"

She flushed bright red and stammered incoherently. Mr Bertram protested, "Really Sergeant, you cannot ask such questions of my mother's staff!"

"Sorry, Sir," said the Sergeant. "You're quite correct. I should leave that to my superiors." He nodded contritely, but I had the impression he had seen the reaction he needed to confirm his suspicions.

"Sergeant," I began, "there was a point I was trying to make earlier."

"Did you ever hear such impertinence," snapped Mrs Wilson, recovering.

"Indeed, Miss, and what might that be?"

"I only wanted to say that the reason, on reflection, I thought the break-in in my room was a break-out – as it were – was that when I discovered the body I do not think it . . . he . . . had been long dead."

"And why do you think that, Miss?" interrupted the Sergeant.

I dug my nails into my palms to keep my patience and took a short breath in. I realised everyone in the room was now regarding me intently. "Because he was still warm," I replied. "Everyone knows a body grows cold with death."

"Do they?" inquired Mrs Wilson. "*You* do."

"Anyone who has ever killed a chicken knows this," I snapped. Mr Bertram's moustache twitched again. "What I am trying to say is that it was very chaotic on the ground floor. I heard screaming. Miss Richenda was arriving. Mr Holdsworth was summoning the police on the telephone. The kitchen was in the midst of serving dinner."

"You're saying that the chaos of the downstairs floors may have driven the assailant upstairs, Miss?"

"Exactly, Sergeant."

"Dear God," breathed Mr Bertram. "The man might have been here all that time? Why did no one think of searching the house?"

No one answered him. Mrs Wilson cast her eyes down.

"A very interesting point, Miss. And a clever one if I may say so. I'm not sure I hold with serving girls being clever," he said darkly, but I was sure I saw his eyes twinkle.

"No, indeed not," affirmed Mrs Wilson, "quite unsuitable."

"Are there passages that lead upstairs, Sir?" asked the Sergeant.

"There's a whole blasted network of passages, Sergeant. I doubt any of the family knows their full extent. It was my father's architect's idea. Damn the man!"

"Sir!" Mrs Wilson was scandalised.

Personally, I found his display of emotion refreshing after the pent-up poker faces of the other gentlemen.

"There should be a copy of the house blueprint in here. Father had it made up into a book. Let me look." Mr Bertram searched the shelves first by running his fingers along the backs of titles, but after a few minutes it was clear the hunted book was not in evidence. At this point he began to pull books from the shelves and toss them on the floor. "Might have hidden the thing," he grunted while heaving a particularly large tome onto the sofa.

I gazed at the Sergeant in horror as book after book tumbled from its rightful place. "Perhaps, Sir, there might be someone who was more familiar with the tome and its whereabouts?" enquired the Sergeant politely as he neatly sidestepped a small avalanche of books from the chaise that were about to land on his boots.

Mr Bertram paused, slack-jawed. "Of course," he cried, "what an imbecile I am! My sister reorganised the library shortly before she moved to the metropolis. I'll fetch her."

And putting action to the thought he strode out of the room in a most commanding manner. I would have been more impressed if he had left less devastation in his wake. I was fairly certain who would be called upon to clear up the mess.

"I think, Mrs Wilson, that now might be a suitable time to interview this Merry."

"Of course, Sergeant. Euphemia, if you could quickly straighten this room. Try as well as you can to put the books back where they belong. I will not expect perfection." With a gracious nod, she steamed out of the room, the Sergeant in her wake.

I sighed and surveyed my surroundings. It had taken Mr Bertram a bare few minutes to wreck this room, but it would take me a lot longer to put it back together. Mrs Wilson might not expect perfection, but if any family member complained they were unable to locate a book, I knew she would take great delight in blaming me. Accordingly, I determined to put everything back in its exact place.

I was half way through reorganising a section on classics that had mysteriously become mixed with turf almanacs – I was developing a suspicion that the master of the house might be more into appearance than actual knowledge – when I heard footsteps. I glanced over at the door-handle and saw it turn. It was true that staff were not meant to be seen generally by the family – we were meant to be some kind of invisible benevolent fairy army that swept, cleaned and generally made their lives perfect – but I was not keen to re-enter the passage where I had found Cousin George. On the other hand, it might be someone seeking me. Or it might be someone coming to retrieve the architect's plans for their own nefarious reasons.

The thoughts flashed through my brain like lightning. Before I could form a solid conclusion, the door was opening. I dived into the small gap behind the screen, narrowly avoiding knocking it to the ground as I pulled it in close.

Footsteps entered the room. I stealthily steadied the screen hoping the new occupant would be looking the other way. Then I crouched down and put my eye to the gap above one of the screen's hinges. It was Mr Richard.

He closed the door quietly behind him and turned the key. My heart turned over. I prayed he had no idea I was here.

He walked directly towards the screen. Then veered off to the fire. I slunk to the edge of the screen and watched from the gap between screen and shelves. To my amazement, I saw Mr Richard stretch up onto tiptoe and run his hands along the top of the mantelpiece. A cloud of dust rolled over him and he began to sneeze violently. But apart from discovering the ineptitude of his mother's staff, he unearthed nothing else. Eyes streaming, he staggered back, then he went down on his hands and knees and began searching the room. I edged as far back against the shelving as I could. My shoes were dark and nondescript. Maybe he would take them as shadows.

Mr Richard checked under the chaise and the wing-chair. Then he checked down the sides of the chair. I could only imagine he was losing his patience because there is no other word than to describe his next actions as ransacking the desk. He pulled out whole drawers and threw them onto the floor. I could not help but reflect he was unlikely to be the brightest member of the family as his secret search was raising quite a commotion.

He turned his attention to the shelves next and began pulling out book after book. I marvelled that he had so far ignored the screen. He stopped, rang his fingers through his hair and turned on the spot surveying the room. Then, of course, he made directly for the screen.

A thousand useless excuses flitted through my brain. That I might appeal to the man's better nature did not occur to me. He was here for a nefarious purpose of that I had no doubt.

He was almost upon me when the door handle rattled loudly. "Hie there! Open the door!" cried Mr Bertram's voice. Mr Richard's head jerked round. Then he fled – there is no other word for it – he fled through the servants' passageway.

I ran over to the desk and quickly fitted the drawers back in place. I had no time to do more. Then I unlocked the door.

"Euphemia! What are you doing?" began Mr Bertram, but then he caught sight of the room behind me. "Did I do all that?" he asked with amazement.

"Not exactly, Sir," I answered honestly. "But you know how it is when one is tidying. It always looks worse before it looks better."

"How very thrilling," said Miss Richenda,

entering the room twirling a long string of beads between her fingers, "a maid who says 'one'. You must come and dress me this evening and tell me more about your humble beginnings."

"Richenda, I hardly think . . ."

"Don't be a tiresome patrician, Bertram. Helping me dress will be a lot better than swilling out the pigs or whatever else Wilson makes our prettiest maids do. Besides, Euphemia and I are old friends. We bonded dragging Cousin Georgie out by his legs."

"Richenda, this is no joke!"

"Darling, the joke is on you. There is no way I could find anything in this mess. Let me know when it's tidied and I'll come back. Right now, I need to go and do service to your dearest Mama. She hasn't made up her mind yet if it will annoy our Papa more if I stay or if I go."

With that she left. Mr Bertram looked at me uncomfortably. "Will you be all right doing all this?"

I curtsied rather than pointing out I had little choice in the matter.

"I don't suppose you have much choice," he said, surprising me. "Nevertheless in this household it would not be appropriate or wise of me to help you."

"No, indeed, Sir," I said, wondering what on earth he meant.

Still he hesitated. "But you are so very small."

I bridled at this. "I am an adequate height for my age and sex, Sir, besides being strong, healthy and young. I assure you any of the tasks that might be reasonably expected of me are not beyond my abilities or talents."

This was quite true as long as no one asked me to boil an egg. I have always been a complete disaster in the kitchen. Mother disapproved of her daughter learning to cook.

Mr Bertram laughed. "I believe you might be, Euphemia. I shall leave you to it." He started to leave and then stopped, his hand on the door handle. "You know," he said over his shoulder, "you really should seek a different situation." And then he was gone before I had a chance to protest.

Mere moments after he closed the door behind him, it opened to admit Mrs Wilson. "You call this putting the room to rights, girl? If this is your idea of decent work . . ."

"It will all be sorted, Mrs Wilson," I promised. "Mr Bertram was here not a moment before you giving me specific instructions." I didn't mention these were instructions to leave.

Mrs Wilson snorted through her nose and turned on her heel. I took this as permission to proceed and did so. It was many weary hours later that I had returned the library to some form of normality. My father would have been appalled by their cataloguing system. I had begun to right this as I worked, until it became apparent it would take the better part of a week to get the contents truly in order. I strongly doubted that, even if I spent the time, any member of the household would appreciate my efforts. So although it went against my natural inclinations, I completed my work within the day. At least the sections were roughly grouped.

I made my way below stairs. Mrs Deighton grabbed me almost immediately. "You sit down there, girl, and you eat. You're far too thin." She sat me at the kitchen table and heaped tubers, bread, gravy and sausages onto my plate.

"But the family . . ." I protested.

"Lord love you, duck," replied the cook. "You've missed all your meals today and goodness only knows when we'll all be sitting down again proper the state the house is in. You get that inside you before they call you up for service."

I was intent on scraping up the last of Mrs Deighton's delicious gravy when a bell began to ring. Shrill and persistent; I imagined the owner was most impatient. Naturally the Butler would know all the bells by sound. My eyes searched the room until I found the bell panel above the main door. It was Miss Richenda. I scrambled to my feet and ran up the servants' stairs.

"I thought you had quite forgotten me." Miss Richenda was seated at her dressing table in a floral dressing gown. Her hair was wet from her bath. With a sinking feeling I realised I was expected to style it.

"Something simple tonight. I don't want dear Step-Mama to have an excuse to say I am dressing like a peacock. But one has to put on a good show. Especially when there's been a murder in the house."

I didn't see why this should be so, but kept my eyes down. "The orange crêpe with the diamanté shoes. Damn dress makes me look twice my age, but Papa likes it."

I dutifully fetched the clothes and helped her into them. Then it was time to do her hair. Fortunately, Miss Richenda, like most women with unflattering hair, knew exactly how it needed to be styled and gave explicit instructions. It was thick like my own but coarser with an animal-like texture. I found styling it highly unpleasant.

"So," said Miss Richenda, her eyes meeting mine in the mirror and holding them, "where did you spring from? You can tell me the truth. I campaign for the woman's right to vote, you know. You have no need to tell me that all the wrongs in the world can be laid at a man's door. What happened to you?"

"My father died and I was left without a penny."

Miss Richenda nodded. "There's a bit more to it than that though, is there not, me dear? Who was your father? Dearest Step-Mama will have it you were born on the wrong side of the blanket. I did myself no favours pointing out a noble bastard was still several degrees more noble than any of us." She gave a barking laugh. "I've been defending you. You owe me the truth. Besides, I'm the only one you can trust."

"Miss?"

"I arrived after the murder."

"Did you hear someone ransacked my room, Miss?"

"I know a distraction when I hear one, Euphemia, but no, I did not."

"It was on the night of the murder. I was next door with Merry."

"Hmm, Merry. She was terribly upset. I wonder . . ."

"It's been an odd sort of day, Miss. What with that book going missing from the library."

Miss Richenda tossed her head. The sudden movement made me stab my finger with a hairpin. "Sorry," she said, but I knew from her expression she didn't care in the slightest.

"Mr Richard was looking in the library too. He made a great deal of mess." I had the satisfaction of seeing her eyes narrow.

"It is not your place to criticise my twin," she said sharply. "He might not be the best or the most careful business man, but he is my twin."

"Oh, I didn't realise Miss," I said. I did not feel I could directly ask about Mr Richard's failings, but I needed to keep the conversation flowing. "You are not that alike. Although I suppose both you and Mr Richard are more akin to each other than to Mr Bertram."

Miss Richenda nodded. "He's dearest Step-Mama's son. Papa's second wife."

"Oh, I thought . . ." I stopped, blushing.

"Oh no," said Miss Richenda, "he married her quite young. My mother died when I was seven. A society beauty, but with a background in trade. We're all terribly middling despite what dearest Step-Mama pretends. This huge house was all her idea."

There was a tap at the door. Mrs Wilson entered. "Euphemia! You are needed. I'm sorry, Miss Richenda. This maid should not be here."

Richenda gestured at the door. "We're done. You can go."

I followed Mrs Wilson out. "Seeing as you are up here, you can clean the upstairs bedrooms. Quickly now. It must be finished by the time dinner is over."

What about mine? I thought, but had the

sense not to say. The labours of a servant were giving me the most enormous appetite. I could only hope the generous Mrs Deighton would remember me. Mrs Wilson opened a small, well-concealed cupboard and thrust a dustpan, brush and duster into my hands.

"Where do I start?"

Mrs Wilson made a sweeping gesture along the corridor. "All the bedrooms on this wing need dusting. Merry should have straightened the beds, but I am making it your responsibility to see that when the family return from dinner they find their rooms in perfect order."

I swallowed, but nodded. My brief acquaintance with the Staplefords gave me little hope they were capable of picking up even a pin.

Mrs Wilson glided away, a dark, self-satisfied apparition. The kinder side of my nature wondered how any woman could have lacked, to such a glacial degree, the warmth of human kindness – what had happened to her to make her such as she was? My other side, the one my mother had worked so hard to suppress, wanted to kick her down the stairs.

To put temptation out of range I chose a room at random and opened the door.

I walked into a bedroom resplendent with heavy, masculine furniture. All the pieces were made from dark-stained wood with a twisted pole detail. The bed was a half-tester with verdant drapery. Curtains of a similar colour and material adorned two wide windows that overlooked the drive. To one side of the bed was a clothes stand with a man's day clothes neatly hung upon it. I recognised the jacket at once as belonging to Mr Bertram. There were two high chests of drawers. Both shut. A dressing table with a hair brush, a small box and a bowl for change was perfectly arranged. A pair of chairs were placed with mirror symmetry at forty-five degree angles either side of the bed. Nothing was out of order, except the green counterpane which was in considerable disarray. The faint smell of a musky, male cologne hung in the air.

It felt impolite to even look for dust in such an immaculate room. I left the dust-pan and broom by the door and began to waft the feather duster. I wasn't entirely sure of its purpose except as a means to move dust from one area to another. Was I meant to sweep it onto the floor and then capture it with the dustpan? It was hardly the kind of question I could ask. Any of the servants would know I was a fraud at once, whereas I was certain should I ever be on chatting terms with the family they would have no idea either.

I reasoned that as long as I went through the motions I had seen all maids do, an acceptable outcome would occur. I set to with a will and quickly discovered that flicking the feather duster was actually quite enjoyable. In Miss Richenda's room there was going to be a lot of work tidying and replacing items, but it was pleasurable to whisk around this near perfect room removing a very few specks of dust and leaving it in totally immaculate order.

I felt I was quite getting into the swing of things when disaster struck. The top of the tester was quite out of my reach, but if I stood on tiptoe I was certain I could reach its sides. I managed to remove a loop of spider-web, but in doing so I dislodged a small dust kitten from further up the bed. I stretched a tiny bit more and over reached myself.

The dust kitten fell on my head and I fell onto the bed sneezing violently.

My impact with the counterpane was hard and painful enough that I didn't even fuss about the mess in my hair. Instead, I rolled over onto my side groaning. The bed was once again soft. There was something hard under the cover. I paused for a moment to collect myself and became aware of a subtle, but distinct male scent coming from the unmade bed. Instead of feeling repelled as a girl of my breeding should have done, I confess I rather liked it. The total impropriety of my response brought me to my senses and I sat up, blushing vividly.

My hand touched the hard surface under the covers. I was here to make the bed, so surely . . . I threw back the counterpane and uncovered a book. The cover was bound in blue leather. Stenciled on the front was the title *The Complete Architecture Drawings of Stapleford House*.

I was kneeling on the rumpled bed, staring down in horror at my discovery when the bedroom door opened and Mr Bertram entered.

Striking a Deal

"What the hell are you doing in my bed?"
demanded Mr Bertram, his face suffused with
colour.

"I am not *in* your bed," I retorted hotly. "I
am *on* it. And pray, what are you doing with the
missing book?" I attempted to brandish the tome at
him, but it was too heavy. I had to content myself
with waggling the hard cover in a way I intended
to be forceful and menacing, but I confess it was
not entirely successful.

"Leave my chambers at once!"

"It is hardly 'chambers'. There is only one
room!"

Mr Bertram walked across to the bed. "There
is an en-suite," he said icily. "One I assume you
were sent to clean rather than rifling through my

possessions."

"I am not rifling!" I protested. I scrambled to the edge of the bed. Mr Bertram was very close, but at least I was no longer among the sheets. "Do not change the subject. You should not have this."

"How dare you tell me what I can or cannot do, wench!"

"I am not a wench," I screeched. "If you do not immediately tell me why this book is hidden in your room I shall scream the place down."

"Euphemia, that is enough."

"I will."

We stood facing each other, eyes locked. I had to look up, but I am sure my intent showed in my eyes because Mr Bertram suddenly gave a huge sigh and seemed to shrink a little. I was conscious of a pang of sympathy. "You are the most extraordinary maid I have ever met," he said, backing towards one of the chairs and sitting on it.

I was about to reply with a blistering retort about so-called gentlemen who sit in the presence of a lady, when I remembered my situation. So instead I drew myself up to my full height and said, "I may be only a maid, but I am a female. Would it be unreasonable of me to expect you to offer me a seat before we talk?"

He waved his hand at the other chair. "Are

we going to talk?"

I sighed and walked round the bed to fetch the other chair. He made no move to help me. I lugged it over. "I do hope you generally treat ladies better than this."

"I am not in the habit of entertaining ladies in my bedchamber."

I flushed.

"I repeat my question, are we going to talk?" he said. This time his moustache was not quivering. It was quite still. His forehead was wrinkled in an unbecoming frown.

I plonked my chair into place and sat down. "You shouldn't frown like that," I said directly, "your hair will recede early."

Mr Bertram put his hand up to check his hairline. I think it was an involuntary action. I suspected from the neatness of the room he was a somewhat vain man. Although I admit I prefer a neat man to an untidy one. But I had what I wanted; I had him off guard. I continued. "I think considering what I have just found concealed in your room, we need to discuss the matter."

"What? Are you going to blackmail me?"

I almost shot out of my chair. "Of course not," I spat. "What do you take me for?"

"I'm not entirely sure what you are. I am fast coming to the conclusion you are no serving maid."

"I think I had already told you that a change in circumstances had led me to seek a position in service," I responded with as much dignity as I could muster.

Mr Bertram grunted. My disgust must have shown in my face for he said, "If you choose to hire yourself out as a maid you will have to become used to men treating you like a servant. I should take this opportunity to warn you that any other male member of the household finding a pretty servant in . . ." I gave him a furious glare and he corrected himself, "*on* his bed would have been unlikely to have behaved with the restraint I have shown."

I quailed inwardly, but I also noted he referred positively to my appearance. "I was led to understand this was a gentleman's household."

Mr Bertram shook his head. "You have no idea of what it means to be a gentleman in these changing times." I opened my mouth to speak. He raised his hand commandingly to silence me and continued. "And you have certainly no idea of what being in service is liable to require of you." He pulled his brows close and leant forward. His eyes travelled from my toes to my head. I felt myself flinching under his gaze. "This is an unsuitable occupation for you."

"So you have said at wearisome length. But what you have not done, Sir, is explain the presence of this book."

Mr Bertram sat back in his seat. "You are akin to a terrier with a rat," he said, smiling slightly.

"Thank you for the flattering comparison," I responded. "I assure you I am a most assiduous hunter."

He did laugh at that. "My god, to be threatened by a maid in my own house! I take it you think I murdered dear Cousin George?"

I considered this idea briefly. I can honestly say it had not occurred to me. I began to realise what a dangerous position I might have put myself in. "No," I said carefully, "I do not think that. However, I do think you had a reason for removing the book. I also would not have described you as overwhelmed by grief. I surmise you know something about this incident you are unwilling to share with the police force."

Mr Bertram clapped twice. "Bravo! You surmise correctly."

"Don't mock me," I snapped. I recovered quickly and added, "Please, Sir."

"What is your interest in all this?"

"It has been variously suggested that I may have some personal involvement with the recent tragedy."

"You want to clear your name?"

"I'm certainly keen not to be dismissed without references."

"So you would not claim you had an innate passion for justice?"

"I have never had cause to consider it," I responded honestly. "Though I naturally would not want a criminal to go unpunished."

"Naturally."

"You don't believe me?"

"I cannot say I am used to having an honest staff. In my experience servants do not tend to mourn the passing of their masters and are more likely to avail themselves of his boots on his demise than weep with grief."

"Then they must have had to endure some very poor masters."

Mr Bertram bowed his head in acknowledgment. "There is merit in what you say. However, while the lower classes may distrust the upper, the upper, or in my case the upper-middle, tend to be wary of the police."

"Scandal," I conjectured.

"Yes, that. An unwillingness to have one's affairs paraded for the amusement of the common lot. But also perhaps a distrust of a police service that is comprised of men who would never be able to afford to live as we – my family – do."

"You think Sergeant Davies is not an honest man?"

Mr Bertram shrugged. I shuddered. "What now?" he asked.

"Now you tell me who you are shielding."

We locked eyes once more. Then to my surprise, he conceded. "Lord knows I have no one else to address my suspicions towards. I shall of course deny this conversation took place if you are ever foolish enough to mention it to another."

"Of course," I responded. "You are a gentleman."

He coloured, but whipped back, "And you are a servant."

"We approach the situation from different sides, but I suspect not entirely different moral stances."

"Madam, you accuse me of having morals?"

"Do not joke, Sir. I acquit you of dishonesty and accuse you of a desire to protect. Who are you shielding?"

"My half-sister, Richenda. My family are an odd lot, but I like her the best of them all."

"And your liking of her would make her murdering of your cousin acceptable? I see now why you and the police force are unlikely to agree."

"You don't understand. I do not know that Richenda did this – and if she has I would not approve of her actions – but there are mitigating circumstances. You would not understand."

"You mean the man was a cad?"

"I see my cousin's epitaph is already being written by rumour. An epitaph is . . ."

"I know what it is," I interrupted. "So your cousin was close to Miss Richenda?"

He pursed his lips. "Let us just say I have always thought it was not only politics that caused Richenda to flee the house as soon as she was able."

"I don't understand."

"Until recently Cousin George lived here."

"Ah, I do understand."

"I rather hope you don't," said Mr Bertram unexpectedly.

"But she arrived after the murder."

"The perfect alibi."

"If you count it being physically impossible for her to have committed the atrocity, yes. I would call that the ultimate alibi. I believe it is also technically known as innocence."

"But did she arrive afterwards?" asked Mr Bertram. He got up and went over to the rumpled bed and threw back the untidy sheets. I tensed myself ready to run, but all he did was uncover and open the book. "Look here."

I crossed cautiously to the other side of the bed. He observed my progress with a wry smile. "If I had nefarious designs upon you, Euphemia, I would not have warned you. Nefarious means . . ."

"I know what it means," I snapped.

He looked at me levelly. "Of course you do. Now come round here where you can see properly."

I gripped my duster firmly. The stick was quite strong and if necessary I could always give him a hearty whack. I came round to his side and stood a shade out of arms' reach. But Mr Bertram showed no sign of wanting to grab me. Instead he opened the book and pointed to a map showing a passage that ran in from the side of the house, connected to the servants' staircase and thus through to the passage serving the library. "I believe this is what they call a discreet entrance. It would have been possible for Richenda to enter from the side of the property and then gain access to the library. She could even retreat the way she had come without being seen and then arrive at the front door."

"Would not the side-door be locked?"

"I doubt it. This is the middle of the country and this is a gentleman's house. It is unlikely that someone would attempt to rob the house during the day. At night, of course, it is more likely and that door would definitely be locked. My father has a very fine porcelain collection that could be targeted by thieves, but even the bravest thief would surely flinch at a daylight robbery. Whereas Richenda . . ."

"Could always say she had slipped in this

way to surprise your parents if she was caught."

"I was going to say Richenda has never lacked courage, but you are quite right, if accosted Richenda could claim she had every reason to be in the house."

"It would still be a bold plan."

Mr Bertram nodded. "But not impossible, you will agree."

"You called it a discreet entrance?"

Mr Bertram fingered his collar. "I should perhaps have called it a discreet exit. I suspect the architecture of this building includes this passage so the master of the house could slip away to see his . . . er . . . local female acquaintance without the Mistress of the house being aware of his absence."

"But this house is not very old . . ."

"Exactly. Another reason I prefer not to show this map to the police. I do not inquire into my father's affairs and I would prefer it if no one else did."

I struggled mentally with this information. That one's father should be such a reprobate! What would it do to the children of the house? How would their young minds be formed under such a situation? If his father had had this discreet exit built into his home, it was not unreasonable to assume this was not a recently acquired predilection. Mr Bertram's voice interrupted my thoughts.

"So do I have your word you will not mention this to the police?"

I stepped back. "I cannot do that."

"Have you no loyalty?" he cried.

"I have been in this house less than twenty-four hours and I would not say it has been a happy experience."

"You are in our employment!"

"You do not buy loyalty, Mr Bertram," I said haughtily. "You might buy silence, but not loyalty."

Mr Bertram reached into his inside coat pocket. "I thought you better than this. How much?" he asked wearily.

"What price is your honour?"

His face positively glowed at that. "My honour is not for sale," he barked.

"And neither is mine," I said quietly.

He gestured to me to take a seat again. "We appear to have reached an impasse."

"Not necessarily. Am I incorrect in thinking that if the murderer should transpire to be other than your step-sister you would want justice to be served?"

"George was an annoying little tick, but . . ." Mr Bertram broke off. "I am not entirely of a mind that there is a but. In many ways whoever rid the world of Cousin George is to be commended."

"It is the hand of God alone who should decide who lives or dies!" I exclaimed.

"Or a jury of twelve good men tried and true?"

"Well, yes. There is that," I conceded. Mr Bertram was a most annoying man.

"Besides, Euphemia, my father is involved in some business deals which I think I say without fear of compromise are at the heart of the nation's interest."

"So now you are saying that rather than bringing scandal to your family the police may choose to conceal the truth? You confuse me, Sir."

Mr Bertram took out his pocket watch. "I confuse myself, Euphemia. Let us say that while I believe the police would be unwilling to look the other way in the face of actual evidence, influence may be brought to bear to close the case quickly, discreetly and without too deep an inquiry."

"But that is wrong!"

"From a moral standpoint I agree, but as a member of the family, should this have been Richenda taking her revenge, I cannot be other than grateful that she will not hang for it."

"But what if it was not her?" I persisted.

Mr Bertram rose, shutting his watchcase with a snap. He frowned heavily. "You really are a most annoying girl and I am late for dinner. I only came to find another pair of cuff links. The chain of this one is broken." He took a broken pair of jade set links from his pocket. "And I find myself embroiled in an ethical and moral dilemma."

"Please go," I responded, quite forgetting myself. "A small thing like justice should never get in the way of fine dining."

The frown vanished in a laugh. "I have been a staunch devotee of Mrs Deighton ever since I was old enough to sneak into her pantry by myself and steal one of her currant buns, but I shan't call her handiwork fine dining. Hearty and wholesome is a more fitting description."

I jumped to my feet and stamped my foot. "By all means put pies before justice!"

At this Mr Bertram laughed even harder. "My dear girl, this has been the most trying of times, but you positively inspire me. I confess in part my unwillingness to come forward with this book has been due to my inability to trust anyone. You, on the other hand, are undoubtedly trustworthy. And again I suggest you are quite in the wrong situation."

"I have little choice, Sir," I responded through gritted teeth.

"Then, I feel you will be a most refreshing addition to the household."

"But the book!"

"Euphemia, I must go!"

"But Sir!"

Mr Bertram sighed. "I offer a compromise. I suggest we pool our obvious intelligences and see what we can discover between us. That neither of us approach the police without fully appraising the other of what we have learned."

"You are proposing we act as a team?" I was astonished.

"Obviously, some of Richenda's ideals must have rubbed off on me. And you have access to the servants' hall and their gossip as I do not."

"If Mrs Wilson has me dismissed I will feel I must reveal what I know before I leave."

"So this is your idea of not blackmailing me? Shame Euphemia!" I could not meet his eyes. "Very well," continued Mr Bertram, "while we are engaged upon this enterprise I will ensure that you stay on staff. I am not entirely sure how I will do so, but I will."

"Thank you, Sir," I said and curtsied.

"Don't curtsy to me, Euphemia. I do not believe you." On which obscure utterance, he threw his broken cuff links into the tray on the dressing table. He then opened the small box and extracted a small silver set. He fitted these into his shirt without a word. Indeed, if we had not but recently been in deep conversation I would have thought him ignorant of my presence. My heart sank as I gained yet more understanding of what it was to be a servant. Mr Bertram completed his task, shut his cuffs and checked his appearance in the mirror. Apparently satisfied with what he saw he turned to exit the room without so much as a glance in my direction. I felt his snub as a dull pain in my solar plexus. It was not unlike indigestion and perhaps appropriately so as he was forcing me to swallow the unpalatable nature of my situation.

As he opened the door, he threw over his shoulder, "Do not forget to clean my bath, Euphemia. I want it to sparkle."

Unfortunately, as I as yet had no idea where such cleaning stuffs were stored, I was unable to do more than dust it. Being a man, I doubted he'd notice the difference.

Gentlemen

I had spent far too long talking to Mr Bertram. I could only hope the family would take their time over dinner. I literally ran from room to room dusting lightly and unfortunately not being able to make the most of my opportunity to understand a little more about the Staplefords.

I do not mean I intended to rifle the bedchambers as Mr Bertram had accused me of doing to his, but now I had the sanction of one of the family to investigate I felt he would not object if I took the time to 'notice' things. However, this would have to wait for another day.

I had barely escaped onto the servants' stairs when I heard the sound of female voices heading upstairs. I surmised they were retreating to the upstairs withdrawing room, but I thought it more than likely that various family members would also choose to return to their rooms for this or that. Already I had an impression of the family as a secretive lot, who preferred to do much of their own fetching and carrying of personal items. It was a condition I was hardly going to contest, but at the same time it strengthened my feeling that this was not a happy house and that it was full of secrets. Really, if it wasn't for the raw and rather biologically explicit aspects of the murder, I would have been finding the whole experience rather exciting, rather like an exceptionally good after dinner puzzle. However, lugging a freshly dead body along a corridor had rather put a damper on the whole business for me.

I presented myself to Mrs Wilson downstairs with a feeling of accomplishment. In return she introduced me to the mending room, where I sat late into the night darning sheets. Fortunately, as my mother had thought it essential that a young woman of breeding be capable of extremely neat hand-stitching and had at almost every opportunity sought to ensure my embroidery progressed, I found the luxury of the comparatively large stitching used in darning both slightly decadent and liberating. It was certainly easy, if lengthy, work.

By the time the female staff were expected to retire I had made significant progress. Mrs

Wilson hardly knew whether to be pleased at the work achieved or dismayed at the abilities of her most despised member of staff.

I conjectured that she would have her revenge. I was not wrong. The next morning I rose early with the rest of the staff and set about laying the fires. Naturally, I expected my first family duty of the day would be to take Miss Richenda a hot cup of tea in my capacity as temporary Lady's maid. Accordingly, I presented myself to Mrs Deighton in good time to collect her morning tray.

The good cook seemed unable to look me in the eye. "Oh well, dearie, I don't know. I think Merry will be taking that up this morning."

I smiled sunnily. The last thing I wanted to do was to step on anyone's toes in the strange internal hierarchy of the servants' hall. "Not to worry, Mrs D," I said in what I hoped was a suitably anything-I-can-do-to-help voice. "I haven't seen Mrs Wilson, but I'm sure she'll have things for me to do."

"She'll be with the Mistress," explained the cook. "Getting her orders for the day. Not that they won't change at least seven times before lunch. Our good Lady Stapleford likes to keep the servants on their toes."

I smiled encouragingly, hoping she would say more and feeling rather like one of those grinning clowns at the travelling festivals. I could only hope my attempt at sunny charm did not look as idiotic as it felt. It seemed to be working.

The cook sighed. "Not like our first Lady Stapleford. Mrs Stapleford, of course, she was first. The Master got his title for helping the nation in the wars."

"Did Sir Stapleford serve in the first Boer war?" I asked, trying to keep the amazement out of my voice.

Mrs Deighton laughed. "Lord love you ducks. The Master is many things, but he's no soldier. No, me dear. Something to do with finance and his bank helping out the government I think. All I knows is he told me a grateful nation was repaying its debt in kind and how did I fancy working for a baronet?" The cook stopped and gazed thoughtfully into the past. "The party we had. They all came, all the leaders of finance and industry and Mrs Stapleford – the new Lady Stapleford looked lovely. We were in the London house then. It was so hot we threw open the long windows. They danced till dawn. I always said it was the mist rising up from the river that did it."

"Did what?"

"Brought on that chill wot killed her. Fiery tempered woman my first Mistress, but heart of gold. Worked for half a dozen charities, both before and after the barony was given. There was some 'as said she was aiming for it, but they had it all wrong. Heart of gold that woman had. Oh, she had a temper like any fire-headed beauty, but she was a kind woman. Not been anyone in the family like her since."

A slightly smouldering smell rose up from the kitchen. "Lord love a duck! What is I doing chatting to you, young miss. That's the Master's eggs all spoiled. Away with you, girl! Mrs Wilson will be down any moment and if you've not found work she'll find it for you."

I nodded, wondering what on earth I was meant to do. Dusting? Again?

"Scoot!" added the cook. "Aggie's unwell today."

"I'm sorry," I said, confused. "I hope it is not something serious."

"If you don't get out of here it's liable to be serious for you," said Mrs Deighton darkly.

I understood her comment approximately five minutes later. I was backing out of the kitchen desperately racking my brains for something useful to do that would also allow me to uncover more clues, when I collided with Mrs Wilson.

"Ah Euphemia!" Her facial expression was curious. I wondered if perhaps a pin had been left in the lining of her austere black dress.

"Are you well, Mrs Wilson?" I asked politely.

The expression stretched and it occurred to

me that this could possibly be how Mrs Wilson looked when she attempted to smile. Her next words robbed me of any doubt.

"How kind of you to ask. Indeed I am very well. Unlike poor Aggie. I'm afraid I will need to ask you to help with her duties."

"But she is the scullery maid," I protested weakly. It had taken me less than a day to understand that the position of scullery maid was of less significance than the kitchen cat. Moreover, the cat was never asked to take out the night soil.

"Indeed. I am glad to see you are picking up the structure of the household so quickly. Fortunately for you, my girl, her mother can't afford to lose the income and she's sent her youngest son, Johnny, to cover many of her duties."

Mrs Deighton coughed loudly. The cough sounded rather like 'trouble', but I may have been mistaken as the cook continued to stir the eggs and did not turn around.

Mrs Wilson paused for a moment, staring hard at the cook's back. "Johnny will naturally be doing most of his work with the male staff."

"Male staff?" I interrupted curiously. "I thought there was only Mr Holdsworth."

"Good gracious," gasped Mrs Wilson. "How on earth could we manage such a large house with so few staff?"

I had been wondering this myself, but I kept my mouth shut.

"We have drivers, gardeners, boot boys, valets and on special occasions footmen."

I longed to ask where the footmen were stored in between special occasions.

"However, you will not be meeting any of them. Unless there is a party of note, when you might, only might, see a footman in the kitchen. I keep my girls well away from the male household. The master did not have separate male and female servants' stairs built for nothing!"

Mrs Wilson misread the alarm in my eyes as I realised my list of suspects was growing by the moment. "So if you have any thoughts of finding yourself a husband here I will remind you that Sir Stapleford will not allow any of that to go on under his roof! This is a respectable household."

So many retorts sprang to my mind, but I continued to keep my tongue behind my teeth.

"This morning, Euphemia, I need you to go down to the kitchen garden and collect cabbages and broad beans."

I nodded.

"If you can manage that," added Mrs Wilson on a note of contempt and glided off, her long black skirts trailing behind her.

"You do know what a cabbage looks like, don't you?" asked Mrs Deighton.

"Of course," I said. She handed me a large basket with a large knife in the bottom and pointed me at the garden door. I was picking my way down the muddy path to the side garden when I realised what that had all been about and broke out laughing. Mrs Wilson did not believe I was a maid. She clearly was still holding to her darling idea that I was an immoral female with nefarious tendencies. She did not expect me to be able to spot a cabbage in its raw form. This was a test. Possibly my mother when she had first married my father would have been flummoxed to uncover a cabbage in its raw form, but any member of a poor vicar's family knew about growing garden vegetables.

I found the cabbage patch and set about hacking away with a will. It was most enjoyable. Cabbages do bear a remarkable resemblance to some heads and have about as much sense in them as some people I could mention.

No one had told me how many to collect. I stopped after nine. The basket was getting very full and very heavy. I wandered off in search of the broad bean frame. The kitchen garden was large. Different areas were segregated by neat box hedges. I rounded one corner and was assailed by the fine smells of rosemary and thyme. A really lovely herb garden was growing there. This garden had been laid out in concentric circles with pretty little seats scattered here and there. I spotted lavender pots. Doubtless, this was an area the ladies of the house sometimes visited.

I was standing admiring the view and wondering where exactly I would find beans, when a boy of about twelve, in clothing so muddy it defied description, came into view, closely followed by a youngish man in a rough brown suit. I stepped back out of view behind the hedge. "Come on, Jimmy me lad," said the man in a wheedling voice. "I've got a bright, shiny penny here for you if you can tell me what I need to know."

"I've told you. I don't know nofink!" protested the boy, who clearly needed an operation for his adenoids. "I don't have nofink to do with the Master."

"But you knows people that do. A clever lad like you Jimmy. Bet you're the pet of the staff. A little word here. A little word there. Mr Martin the driver seems a very chatty bloke. Lovely motor he's got. You interested in motors, Jimmy?"

"Of course I'm interested in motors!" piped up Jimmy.

"Well then, it wouldn't be a big hardship to go talking to Mr Martin about the runs he's been on in the car recently, would it?"

"Why don't you ask him yourself?" asked the boy.

"Jimmy, Jimmy, Jimmy. You've got a lot to learn about how the world works lad. You do this little favour for me and I'll give you a bright new penny."

"I still don't understand why you can't ask him yourself."

At this point I revealed my presence. "That is quite correct, Jimmy," I said in my best vicar's daughter voice. "Run along now and leave this man to me."

Jimmy threw me a look that said he thought I had recently escaped from the mad house. However, he was obviously not overly enamoured of the penny-man either and took the opportunity to, I believe the term is, leg it.

"As for you, Sir, I shall not enquire of your business. Anyone who opportunes a child for information is hardly likely to be working for one of our more respectable periodicals."

To give the man credit he did remove his pork pie hat at the sight of me, but his tone was not respectful. "Respectable! Respectable! I like that coming from you!"

"Sir, you know nothing about me!" Goodness, could he be a relative of Mrs Wilson? "I need you to leave now. I have beans to collect."

He approached me pointing a finger in my direction and ignoring my vegetable dilemma. "I'd like to know how you equate respectable with the

death and destruction your family has caused."
He gestured at my basket. "How do you eat? How
do you swallow that knowing your family fortune
is coined from the blood of others?"

I moved backwards as far as I could until the
hedge pressed against me. He kept coming and I
confess I was frightened. "I don't know what you
are talking about," I blurted out. "My father might
have been responsible for sending a number of
men and women to their final rest, but he was no
murderer!"

"Ha! So you admit it!" cried the man. "But
it's not your father I am interested in, but his
son."

It dawned on me then that he had mistaken me
for one of the Staplefords. This lent me strength.
"Leave this garden at once or I shall summon the
police!"

"And how are you going to do that?" The
man sneered showing nasty yellow teeth.

"I shall scream." I replied with dignity. "There
is still a Sergeant at the house."

The man's face contorted in anger. He shoved
his hat upon his head. "Don't you think I will let
this matter rest, Ma'am. You can't stifle the press
no matter who you are. The country don't want
the likes of him in power. You mark my words.
Not when they know the truth . . ."

I took a deep breath. It was enough. I was

gratified to see him beat a hasty retreat across the garden. The beans transpired to be around the next corner, so I was able to fill my basket to the brim and return to the house feeling accomplished. Though I must admit, the newspaper man's conversation, no matter how many times I replayed it in my mind, left me with a considerable number of questions. Regretfully, due to my lapse in commenting on my father's existence, not to mention his propensity to bury the dead, I felt I could not mention the conversation to another in case they tracked down this man and inadvertently exposed my origins.

I entered the kitchen triumphantly bearing my full basket proudly before me. The cook was frantically whipping up something in a bowl. As I came in she stopped, held up the whisk and looked in dismay as a thin line of liquid dribbled from it. I had no idea what she was making, but even I with my limited culinary skills could tell it was not going well. She noticed me and annoyance suffused her face.

"Where have you been, Euphemia!" cried Mrs Deighton. "I need those beans now! Take 'em through the scullery and while you're at it, scrub those cabbages. I hope you got four. You never bothered to ask before you flounced off."

I nodded. I had got four, more than four, but I didn't think now was the time to be pedantic.

"Good. Waste not want not. That's what I always say." Mrs Deighton indicated the scullery with a nod of her head.

It was a dingy little room with only a small window set high up in the wall. There were three bars across it. The scullery had a large, low sink with a cold water pump attached and a big wooden draining board. It managed to have both the most modern of conveniences and the most miserable of ambiances.

I dumped my basket down angrily on the side. I knew, as my father had taught me, that all people were created equal in God's eyes. "All men," I muttered savagely pulling the outer leaves off a poor cabbage. I was aware that even in this house, even between the ranks, there was some camaraderie between the men, but the women, like the poor scullery maid, were all lowly creatures bent on seducing the men and secluded for their own protection against their immoral tendencies.

"Ha!" I cried dumping the shorn cabbage in the sink. I thought of Merry's tear-stained face and her belief in good old Cousin Georgie. Good old Cousin George who might well have taken advantage of Richenda if Bertram's suspicions were correct. This house was a seething morass of . . . of . . . wrongs! Worse than even I suspected if there was any sense behind that newspaper man's incomprehensible accusations.

"Careful there, my pretty, I prefer my vegetables unbruised."

I whirled round to see Mr Richard walking calmly towards me. He hesitated as he peered through the half-light.

"Why you're not little Aggie! I didn't think she was the spirited sort. Not with the vegetables anyway. You're Euphemia, aren't you?"

I did not entirely understand his tone, but involuntarily I edged back against the draining board. I reached behind me into the basket, feeling for the knife.

"So then, I think it is time we got better acquainted," said Mr Richard in a horrid, slimy kind of voice.

My fingers, still somewhat cold from my gathering in the garden, fumbled in the basket. Where was the knife? My numb fingertips scraped along something long and hard. I grasped it quickly. I pulled it out and shouted, "Sir, I am not that kind of a maid!" and flourished a string of beans in his face. I had been so sure it had been the knife.

Mr Richard roared with laughter. "Oh yes, I really must get to know you, Euphemia."

I was trapped. Between me and the first son of the household was only a string of beans and even by this light I could see they weren't very good beans.

"I'll scream," I said, falling back on my favourite defence.

He was too close now. I could smell his cologne. He leant in, there was liquor on his breath. "Do you think anyone will hear? Do you think anyone will care, Euphemia?"

"Sir," announced a sonorous voice from the doorway, "I have found a bottle of the '87. I think your father would infinitely prefer it if you decanted it yourself."

Mr Richard swung round. "I doubt that Mrs Wilson, but I will." He whispered in my ear. "Foiled this time I retire from the lists little maiden, but I shall return."

Mr Richard walked out of the room quite calmly as if nothing had happened at all. I turned and leant over the sink, fighting the urge to be sick. "Thank you, Mrs Wilson," I gasped.

"Might I advise, Euphemia, if you have any other option at all, to seek another position. This is not the right situation for you."

I swallowed down bile as I nodded. "Yes, I am beginning to think you are right," I said and vomited over the cabbages.

Ladies

The next morning I was given the job of taking up Miss Richenda's tray and Merry was sent down the garden. None of the family had commented on any unusual flavours in yesterday's side dishes, but there was a general, if unvoiced, agreement to keep me out of the scullery.

Unfortunately, Miss Richenda rose late in the country, so there was more than ample time for me to sort and fold the linen. This proved to be a tedious and time consuming job. There are really no secrets to be learned from endless piles of clean sheets. However, if Aggie did not soon return I would be given the opportunity of seeing what I could learn from dirty ones. I did not relish the idea. All in all my initial enthusiasm for helping Sergeant Davies and Mr Bertram was at a very low ebb. The ladies of this house were self-centered, unpleasant and idle. The gentlemen, on the other hand, were far from idle enough. The only person among the family for whom I felt the least disliking was Mr Bertram and even he was disagreeably annoying.

I tapped on Miss Richenda's door, so as not to startle her, and entered. I almost dropped the tray. The room was in terrible disarray. As my eyes took in the spilt powder on the dressing table, the items of clothing strewn across the room and the unturned chair I thought the room had been ransacked.

"Miss Richenda!" I called in alarm.

A tousled head appeared from under the bright crimson covers. Richenda eased herself to a sitting position. She cradled her head protectively. "Not so loud, Merry!" She blinked blearily at me. "Oh, it's you. Look out for that chair. Is that tea? Lovely!" Richenda swept the contents of the bedside table onto the floor. A magazine, a beaded necklace and a little notebook joined the chaos below.

I placed the tray carefully on the new space. I hovered, uncertain of what to do. I was beginning to realise it was no stranger who had created this havoc. I must have let too much show on my face, as Miss Richenda frowned. "Merry didn't tell you, did she? About my little problem?"

"No, Miss."

"I sleep walk. Have done since a girl. I don't tend to go far. But as you can see I do tend to leave a trail behind me."

A thought flashed across my mind. I had heard somnambulism was caused by a troubled mind. What was troubling Miss Richenda? "Never mind, Miss. I can clean this up for you dead quick." I could not manage Merry's accent, but I felt my simpler speech was a good imitation of my station.

Richenda nodded. I reminded myself internally that she didn't need to thank me. This was my job. Besides, tidying her things and going through her things were two terribly similar actions.

Miss Richenda slurped at her tea. There is no other word to describe it. The sound was quite revolting, but it seemed to refresh her. Her eyes snapped open. "Where have you been?" she demanded.

"Right here, Miss."

"No. No. Yesterday. I had no maid with me. I was rather expecting you to wait on me."

"I'm sorry, Miss. Mrs Wilson had a lot for me to do."

Miss Richenda screwed up her face. "Ooooh, that wretched woman! She would do anything to spite me!"

She lapsed into contemplative silence.

"I would not want to speak ill of any member of staff," I said quickly. She looked up. I had her attention. "But I think even Mrs Wilson's closest friend would say she is not the easiest lady to work for." Miss Richenda's eyes searched my face. I lowered my eyes. "Such exacting standards," I murmured. Had I gone too far?

Miss Richenda scoffed. "Exacting standards? She likes to think she runs this house."

I thought frantically, but there was really nothing I could reply to this without contradicting her. My confusion must have shown on my face.

"Yes. Yes. I know she technically runs this house, but I mean actually runs it. Dearest Step-Mama gives her the daily orders and she follows them."

"She seems very competent," I said mildly. "She writes all the orders down in a little book."

"Oh yes, she will do things by the letter because then if anyone goes running to my father she can quote chapter and verse back at you. Damn impertinence I call it. I give servants' directions. I mean, you've got a brain, haven't you?"

I nodded.

"Well then, if I said, 'tidy this room' you would go through my things and put them all back in the proper places would you not?"

I nodded again.

"Well, if I tried giving Mrs Wilson an order like that she'd go through every single item checking where each thing should go. It would take so bally long I might as well do the job myself."

I murmured something about being thorough again.

"Rubbish. The woman hates her job. But she won't leave my father."

I had the sense we were edging into dangerous territory. I stayed hopefully silent. Miss Richenda flung out of bed. "I expect you're wondering what I mean by that, aren't you?"

"Yes, Miss," I admitted. I am very bad at lying. I always imagine Father standing beside me shaking his head.

Miss Richenda gave one of her loud barks of laughter. "Don't mince words, do you? Hand me that robe! I'll need you to run me a bath. None of that awful pink stuff in it that dearest Step-Mama insisted on filling the house with. Stinks something awful."

"Certainly, Miss. At once." I made my way slowly enough towards her bathroom to give her as much opportunity as possible to let another indiscretion drop. She did not disappoint.

"She knew my father when he was a young man," she said as I opened the bathroom door.

"He's very fond of her. No accounting for taste."
She hesitated then added in a run, "All the men
in my family are a sight too damn fond of the
servants if you ask me."

I came back into the room. "Miss, I don't
want to speak out of turn, but seeing as you
have mentioned it I'm wondering if I might not
be happier in another situation. Would you be
willing to give me a letter of reference?"

To be honest, I did not know if I wanted to go
or I wanted to stay. There were arguments in both
directions, but I did not think it would harm either
option to have Miss Richenda think I respected
her more than anyone else.

"Tsk! Tsk! Euphemia, a clever girl like you
knows the time of day. We can't be another maid
down. Who will press my dress? Merry made a
hack-handed mess of it yesterday. You leave it to
me. I'll have a word and sort this out. Men need
to be put in their place. I can do that for you."

"Thank you, Miss." The fierce expression
on her face almost made me feel sorry for Mr
Richard. Almost.

I ran her bath. "Perfect, Euphemia. Now, if
you could pick up things a bit in here. And when
you have done that you might like to take a good
look through my wardrobe. It needs a bit of
sorting. Press dresses. Rearrange shoes. That sort
of thing."

This turned out to be an understatement. By the time Miss Richenda had finished her long soak in the tub, I had achieved the impossible and made the room even more of a mess. When I opened the wardrobe I could almost swear clothing had leapt across the room it was so tightly packed in.

Miss Richenda was now fresh as a daisy and I was mired down deep in clothes that should have been sent for cleaning rather than stuffed back in the wardrobe. It wasn't my place to ask how this could have happened, but I did feel she owed me. "Miss? Do you mind if I ask you a question?"

Miss Richenda was powdering her face. Until that moment I had not realised optimism was one of her defining characteristics. Nothing short of paint would be able to cover those freckles.

I shook away the uncharitable thoughts. The lady continued to dab.

"Miss?"

"Yes, what is it Euphemia?"

"I met this strange man in the garden."

"How unwise."

"I think he was a pressman, Miss. He mentioned something about this being a house of death and destruction."

"Sounds more like a tinker trying to sell lucky heather to me."

"You've no idea what he meant, Miss?"

Miss Richenda turned to show me a face of

clown-like whiteness. "Really, girl, you shouldn't waste your time talking to hawkers. Now, tell me, is this too much powder, do you think?"

"No, not all, Miss," I said steadily.

Once she had left I made a thorough search of the room. This wasn't as nefarious as it sounded. It was actually necessary to go through all her possessions to uncover the furniture hidden underneath. That little pocketbook, of which I had been cherishing much hope, provided to me no more than a list of items she required, stockings, face powder and lists of popular songs. It was, I thought unkindly, as empty as her head.

My stomach was reminding me I had been here almost all the morning when the door opened and Merry bounced in. "There you are! Mrs Wilson's in a right lather, you not telling her where you were. The Master wants to see you right now."

I looked down helplessly at my crumpled uniform.

"Right now, Missy, Chop! Chop! Wot 'ave you been up to?"

Merry's bright eyes sparkled with mischief. It was good to see her forgetting her woes, but I could not but feel the situation was unfortunate.

I was not even slightly surprised to see Mrs Wilson waiting for me in the library. Personally, I was less than keen to return to this room, but the housekeeper appeared not to share my qualms. The Master of the house was seated at a desk. A rug, with a bright and dizzying pattern had been thrown over the area where Miss Richenda and I had dragged the body.

As I entered, Sir Stapleford eased his chair back, catching the edge of it on the new rug. "Damn and blast this thing Wilson. Will you have it removed?"

"The Mistress requested it," she said in a pale voice.

"Does the Mistress use this room? Wretched woman barely knows how to read!" stormed the Master of the house in a most ungentlemanly manner.

I dropped a small bobbing curtsy. As I hoped, the movement distracted him.

"What do you want, girl?" he barked.

"You sent for me, Sir," I said politely.

"Did I? Why the hell did I do that?"

"It was about the garden incident, Sir," a thin smile spread across the pallid features. Mrs Wilson, I reflected, had the kind of face that looked better in death. I do not mean I have murderous intentions towards her, rather that having been present at a number of wakes, usually helping with tea for the mourners, I had had the opportunity to see an unusual number of deaths in my time. This memory brought two things to mind. Firstly, why are the bereaved always so thirsty – a question for which I still have no answer. Secondly, no one had made any mention of Cousin Georgie's funeral.

"The odd tasting cabbage?" asked Sir Stapleford.

"The incident with the *man*."

How the woman managed to get such an unpleasant mixture of suggestion and malice into one three letter word is a skill I wish I never succumb to learning.

"Mentioned by Miss Richenda?" Mrs Wilson added.

"Ah, yes. You came across a pressman in the garden?"

"A fine story," snorted Mrs Wilson. "This is the new girl, Sir. On a fortnight's trial. I'm afraid she is not proving suitable."

"Indeed," said Sir Stapleford. "Why not?"

"She shows distressing signs of ideas above her station, Sir."

"Hmm," the Master puffed into his moustache, considering the situation. Then he said, "What happened with the pressman, girl?"

"I do not know he was a gentleman of the press, Sir. It is only what I surmise."

Sir Stapleford's bushy eyebrows rose and I mentally cursed my inability to talk as befitted my new station.

"He was asking the gardener's boy questions about your comings and goings. When I appeared on the scene, the boy took the opportunity to leave. I suggested to the man he might be advised to do likewise. He attempted to ask me some questions, but I rebuffed him."

"Did you indeed?" barked Sir Stapleford. "Did he say anything else to you?"

"He made a comment about the family fortune being founded on death and destruction." Sir Stapleford's expression darkened, so I added quickly. "I have no idea what he was referring to and so I told him and sent him on his way."

"How exactly did you do this?" asked my Master.

"I threatened to scream very loudly, drawing the attention of the Constable I claimed was still in the house, if he did not vacate the premises."

"Ha! Ha!" barked Sir Stapleford. "You've got a rare one here, Jenny!"

The world shifted slightly as I understood Mrs Wilson had a Christian name and so, despite appearances, a cleric must have attempted to drive out the devil at her baptism. You will forgive me if I suggest he must have been young and inexperienced.

"Well done, my girl! Well done!" He rummaged in his trouser pocket. "Come here. I've something for you."

It was with some trepidation I approached. Sir Stapleford handed me a half sovereign.

"Thank you, Sir," I stammered. It was an extraordinary amount of money.

"Now, don't you go mentioning this to any of the staff. Don't want them thinking I'm going soft."

"No, Sir," I said and curtsied.

"Oh, and no reason to mention to anyone what that man said. Only upset me wife and daughter. Least said and all that. Understand, girl?"

"Of course, Sir." I was now burning with curiosity.

"Excellent! Excellent! Don't think this is a case of ideas above her station, Jenny. Strikes me the girl has unusual intelligence. Long as you don't find her in me sons' bed, she'll do. Do you good to have a sensible pair of hands to help you rather than those yokel block heads you normally employ."

Mrs Wilson gave me a look of pure bile. "As you say, Sir. Perhaps Euphemia should leave us now?"

"What? What? You still here, girl? Off about your work. No dillydallying in my house," and he gave me what I can guess he meant as a roughish wink. Fortunately, breakfast had been some time earlier.

I made my way back to the kitchen, my head

in a whirl. A half sovereign! I knew a bribe when I was given one. There were more secrets in this household than nails in a coffin. An unfortunate simile, but as I stepped out into the bright, warm realm of Mrs Deighton I could not shake a deep-seated conviction that unfurled within my very bones that there was more evil to come.

A Clandestine Meeting

I should have somehow sealed the half sovereign to the paper. I should have begged a stamp from Mrs Deighton. I should never have accepted the money in the first place. But as my Father would often say, hindsight is the clearest vision of all and the least helpful.

I had not had the forethought to pack paper and ink with me. I was lamenting this fact in the kitchen when Merry amazed me.

"I have a leaf or two you could borrow if you have to write to your Ma."

I garbled a thank you and promised to replace whatever I used. Merry flushed. "I can write you know," she said lifting her chin high.

"Of course," I muttered, embarrassed she had read my thoughts.

"Writes something lovely, she does," chimed in Mrs Deighton, "makes checking the stores that much easier."

"I'll get it for you," said Merry.

"Oh dear," said the cook, "now I've offended her. I was ever so pleased to help her when she decided she wanted to better herself. But she's so sensitive about it. I keep telling her she's good enough for any nice young bloke, but I don't know . . ." Mrs Deighton trailed off. "I've been worried she'd got herself entangled in something. You've got to be careful in this house, dearie. Have a word with her, Euphemia. She likes you, and Merry, for all her smiles, doesn't take to everyone."

"I'll go after her. I'd rather write my letter upstairs anyway."

"If you're quick about it you'll have time to run down to the post office in the village. I'll tell Mrs W I've sent you for some extra currants. Not much of a lie as someone's been picking at 'em. I reckon Holdsworth has a secret sweet tooth." We both laughed at the thought of the Butler covertly nibbling dried fruits. "Here's a couple of pennies. Now you be quick. You'll only have time to pen a line or two, but your mother will be pleased to know you're safe."

I took the pennies and scampered up the stairs. Merry met me halfway along the attic corridor. "Here," she said, handing me a couple of tissue thin sheets, a small bottle of muddy ink and a rough pen. "Will this do?"

"It's lovely," I lied.

"Do you want an envelope too?"

I nodded. "I'll replace them."

Merry shrugged. "You get writing and I'll bring you one."

I went into my room and sat looking at the paper in dismay. It had been my intention to send the half sovereign to Mother, but the paper was too thin to support my sealing of it and I suspected the envelope would be of similar quality. Worse yet, Merry had liberally sprinkled the pages with lavender water. On the positive side the watermarks were few, but unfortunately the paper reeked. What on earth Mother would make of this I hardly dare imagine. I was certain she would ascribe to the belief that only Women-of-a-Certain-Sort used perfumed paper. I was sniffing the paper when Merry came in behind me.

"Is there a problem?" Her voice was peppery with indignation.

I turned and smiled. "I was thinking how cleverly you had perfumed these sheets." And this wasn't a lie. It wouldn't have been easy for Merry to both make and use the lavender water.

"Cook said I could."

"Could what?" I asked mystified.

"Take lavender from the garden."

"Of course. I didn't think anything else."

"Oh yes you did," said Merry, dumping the envelope down on my desk. "You've been setting yourself above the rest of us."

I blinked at the vehemence in her voice. "Merry," I said gently, "I know this is a terrible time for you."

She cut me off. "I'll have to ask you to replace what you use."

"Of course," I said coldly. "I would not dream of trespassing on your kindness."

Merry gave me a look of pure loathing and flung out of the room. I tried to clear my brain and write a few short lines to Mother.

Dearest Mother,

I hope you are well and that the new cottage is to your liking. I have had to borrow this paper from another maid. I shall procure proper paper soon. I have been fortunate enough to be able to do the master of the house a personal service and have a half sovereign which I shall shortly send to you. The lamentable thinness of this stationery precludes the possibility.

I hesitated. She might hear of the murder. For all I knew it was already in the papers.

If, by any chance, you had heard news of the unfortunate occurrence at this house, please be assured that I am well and under no suspicion. The cook at this house, Mrs Deighton, is a most respectable woman, as is the Butler, a Mr Holdsworth. Both have taken me under their wing and I am quite getting into the swing of working in such a big house. There are adequate servants and I do not find the work hard.

At the first opportunity I will return home for a short visit to assure you of both my health and my good fortune in securing this position.

Your loving, dutiful daughter

Euphemia

Post script: Much love to Little Joe

Post post script: I hope the new pigs are proving obedient and fattening quickly.

I read over the letter.

Post post post script: Mr Holdsworth is, of course, a man, but still quite respectable.

I hesitated.

Post post post post script: Please forgive the post scripts, but this letter was written in haste as I only have a short time to reach the post office before it closes.

It was less than a pattern card letter, but then I had only the two sheets, little time and I knew Mother hated reading a scored through letter. At least I would not be present to hear her strictures on my lackadaisical correspondence. I fitted the letter to its envelope, collected my outdoor things and hurried down the back stairs.

The air was sharp with an impending frost and the winter light weak, but already the turning of the year at midwinter meant daylight lasted a little longer.

I had had more than adequate opportunity to mark the way from my slow arrival on cart and had a fair idea of where the village lay. I also have a remarkable sense of direction, so despite the confusion of copses of trees on both the left and then the right side of a crossroads and the exceedingly bad lettering on the sign, I soon found myself heading down the hill towards the pretty little village green with its crop of cottages and small shops.

The sun was levelling off on the horizon, sending the bare trees with their angular black limbs into sharp relief. A smooth white frost crept across the fields; the white line practically rising before my eyes as if dragged by invisible hands. The air caught at the back of my throat in a not unpleasant manner. The cold pinched my face, rousing my mood and clearing my mind. I was surprised how happy I felt.

Ahead I could see the lane branched once more and then I would be on the direct path into the village. Looking out across the fields I gathered my bearings. I was now fairly certain I could find my way walking across the fields rather than braving the network of lanes. The gathering frost would make walking across the fields easier. This could give me a little extra time. Perhaps enough to discover if there was a village shop that sold those toy soldiers Little Joe so craved.

"Euphemia!"

I turned, startled to see Mr Bertram emerge from the other branch of the lane. Any suspicion he might have been following me was quickly put to flight as his once white and now distinctly muddy wolfhound hurried to meet me.

As the beast leapt I caught his big, dirty paws and controlled the big, friendly brute as he tried to cover my face with dog kisses.

Growing up in a rural vicarage has few advantages, but one of these is the ability to quickly size up the temperament of canines. If only I was able to do the same with their masters.

"Down Siegfried!" shouted Mr Bertram.

The dog showed no signs of obeying him, being happily engaged in trying to lick my face. I laughed and scolded the animal, dropping his paws away from me and earning his love by scratching his ears.

"I see you are used to dogs," Mr Bertram said quizzically. "Very unusual for a London maid."

I smiled at him. "I have never been to London, Sir."

"Indeed? I thought that was perhaps where

you had acquired your polish?"

I laughed then, quite forgetting my place. It was easy to do outside the house. "Indeed not! I am country bred through and through."

Mr Bertram gave me a look I could not fathom. Then he said quite sharply, "We should not be seen together."

This brought me down to earth at once. My happiness evaporated. I bobbed a curtsy. "No, Sir. I am on my way to the post office to post a letter to my mother. If you will excuse me."

I curtsied again and turned to go. Mr Bertram was suddenly at my side. He caught my arm. "No, Euphemia. We should talk, but not in such an unguarded place as this. Do you know the Red Lion?"

I shook my head, bewildered.

"The Inn. It is below us and a little to the right. Take the lane and I will go cross country. I will meet you outside. The snug bar is dark and we can talk there."

"Sir," I stammered, "I cannot go into a public house. I believe most will not even admit women."

"For heaven's sake, Euphemia, you will be with me. The landlord will allow me to bring in who I choose."

"I thought you did not want us to be seen together?"

"You have only to pull up the hood of your cloak until we are seated. No one will know who you are."

"It does not seem right, Sir!"

"Oh, don't be a silly girl, Euphemia. If you were a lady it would be different, but you are a maid. A maid in quite a precarious position in my father's household."

I blushed red. "That is unfair."

"You want to keep your position, don't you?"

"Of course," I responded, "but not at the cost of my virtue."

He laughed loudly at that. "Euphemia, I accuse you of reading novels! You are the most unusual girl. But fear not, I have no designs upon your person, I want only to borrow your mind."

His speech awoke a curious mixture of emotions within me. I could not readily untangle them. I only knew I felt distressed. "I'll meet you," I agreed to bring the uncomfortable scene to an end and set off smartly down the lane.

The bar was very much as he had said. On the outside the Red Lion presented the appearance of a local, but respectable inn. It was built of grey granite blocks and was neatly thatched. It comprised two storeys and the paint work on the windows and doors was neat and fresh.

Mr Bertram arrived very shortly. As we

entered through the side door we immediately plunged into gloom. The bar was small and cramped. Mr Bertram led me to a secluded, tiny bay and went to collect refreshments. I noted the exit.

He left Siegfried, who seemed used to the location, with me. He curled up under the table, but like many large dogs he unfortunately forgot the length of his tail. A large man trod on it and the poor dog yelped. The man cursed us both in unbecoming language, and I forgot myself enough to berate him for his carelessness. I believe things might have gone rather ill if it had not been for a shuffling at the closely packed bar. The man, when offered the choice between arguing with me and getting in his order, chose to head for his ale.

Mr Bertram returned with a half pint of beer for me and a full pint for himself. In response to his "Cheer-ho!" I forced myself to take a sip of the brew. It was vile. "Thank you," I stammered.

He smiled. "Tell me what you have learnt. Be honest. I will not take offence, but keep your voice low."

"Merry was close to your cousin George," I began.

Mr Bertram whistled softly. "So that's how it was."

"No, I do not believe so. Merry had much

affection for the gentleman and believed that a future together was possible. Do not look at me like that Mr Bertram. I am fully aware that he could have had no such intentions towards her. However, I believe Merry had not crossed a . . . er . . . certain line before his death and is possibly the person most emotionally affected by his death."

"So no chance she killed him in a fit of revenge?"

"I do not think so. Obviously, as a servant she had ample knowledge of the various passageways and when I casually enquired of her whereabouts during the actual murder, neither Mrs Deighton nor Mr Holdsworth could give me an answer."

"What about Mrs Wilson?" asked Mr Bertram.

"She is not a person one can make casual enquiries of."

Mr Bertram waved his hand. "No, I know that. She does not like you. I meant did she have opportunity or motive that you know of?"

"Again, I have not been able to verify her whereabouts. Although I imagine the police will be looking into exactly this."

"My father has asked the police to move things along quickly. There is the seat to be taken into account."

"Seat?" I queried. Mr Bertram shook his head. "It's not relevant. Do you think Mrs Wilson could have killed him?"

"I like her as little as she likes me, but unless your cousin George was in some way threatening your father or her own position I cannot see her committing such an act."

Mr Bertram downed a large part of his pint. "We do not appear to be progressing."

I sighed. "When I tidied your step-sister's room I did not come across anything helpful."

"You searched Richenda's room?" Mr Bertram's voice hovered between disapproval and amusement.

"I tidied it, Sir, and it was in sore need of tidying. However, I did learn she has become prey to somnambulism once more. Something I believe she is prone to during times of stress."

Mr Bertram nodded soberly.

"Again, I am afraid I do not have anything to share over Mr Holdsworth's locality during the murder. Except we know he was in position to open the door to Richenda very shortly after the murder was committed."

"The library is not far from the front door," commented Mr Bertram.

"No," I countered, "but although I am not particularly knowledgeable about murders, it seems odd to me that one man could kill another and then calmly go about his duties."

"Unless he was either an actor or had very

good cause for wishing a man dead."

"I know of neither to be true of Mr Holdsworth." I longed to ask him about his thoughts on the family, but I was beginning to understand that my position was to provide information on my peers. The actual term for such an occupation I pushed to the back of my mind.

"Thank you, Euphemia. I can only ask you to keep your eyes and ears open for me. Currently there appear to be many suspects for this murder."

"Do you have any ideas?" I ventured.

"What I think, my dear," said Mr Bertram rising, "is that you should hurry to post your letter. I will hasten back to the hall so our arrivals will not seem to follow too closely upon one another."

I had no wish to stay a moment alone in the inn, so I hastened after him. The post office proved to be only a short distance from the inn. It also proved to be closed. There was a public post box, but I had no stamp. I hesitated. I could pop it in the box and leave the charge to Mother, but considering our shortage of funds I decided against it. I was certain Mother would wish to hear I was doing well, but I was equally certain she would not want to pay for the privilege. I placed the letter back in my coat pocket.

The walk across the fields was pleasant and,

as I had suspected, much quicker. The small frosty puddles snapped beneath my boots as I strode over the muddy fields. Back in the fresh air I felt freer and happier. As long as the family remained at the Hall I could always take pleasure in this temporary escape.

All too soon I was walking up the tree-lined drive to Stapleford Hall. The dusk was drawing in and the trees loomed over me like austere sentries. I have spent most of my life living next to graveyards. Although Papa tried to keep the more morbid side of his occupation from the family, this was impossible. Mother, who was more than happy to do the family visits, hated attending the wakes and I often stepped in. It is perhaps unfair to mention this, but towards the end I was also the one who visited the seriously sick in our parish, Mother having acquired a dread fear of contaminating Little Joe. I digress to mention these facts to prove I do not have an innately fanciful imagination. I do not, as Little Joe often pretends, see ghosts hovering in the air. I had no sense of foreboding when my own father died. Yet, as I walked with increasing reluctance up the tree lined avenue, I had the strangest feeling of darkness gathering all around me. If I had had anywhere else to go, I do believe there might have been a strong chance I would have fled.

As it was, I slipped in through the servants'

entrance. In the kitchen was an unfamiliar constable. He was seated at the kitchen table watching the door through which I had just come, as a cat watches a mouse hole. He rose as I entered.

"Euphemia St John?"

"Yes."

"You must come with me." He crossed the room in two swift strides and grasped me roughly by the arm. "And no funny business."

"Ouch! Let me go! You're hurting me."

"Not likely, girl. I've got you now."

"I'm not trying to escape," I protested. "This must be some kind of misunderstanding."

But he was too intent on dragging me upstairs to listen to my pleas. In fact, other than squeezing my arm in a vice-like grip he paid me no attention at all. I, on the other hand, was able to ascertain his personal hygiene left much to be desired and he had wiry ginger hairs growing out of his ears.

"I've got her, governor!" he yelled as we reached the main hall. "I've got the girl." He stopped, waiting for a response.

"You make it sound as if you have had to chase me over several fields as opposed to merely dragging an unresisting young girl up a few stairs," I said. He continued to ignore me.

Mr Richard stormed into the hall closely followed by Mrs Wilson. Mrs Wilson's face was contorted in a grimace. I realised she was smiling. I began to worry.

"Where have you been, girl?" exploded Mr Richard.

"Down to the village, Sir."

"A fine story!" cried Mrs Wilson.

"Who gave you permission?" thundered Mr Richard.

"Mrs Deighton."

"Why?"

"She wanted me to get some currants," I said in a very small voice. I had completely forgotten my errand.

"So where are they?" cried Mrs Wilson.

"I forgot," I mumbled.

"Nonsense. You never went down to the village at all, did you?"

"I did!" I protested.

"Then how comes your boots aren't muddy?" asked the constable.

"The frost is coming down," I snapped. "Will you kindly let go of my arm? I'm not liable to run away."

"Empty your pockets," asked Mr Richard more calmly.

Puzzled, I turned out my coat pockets. My letter was ignored, but Mr Richard pounced on the coin and held it up in front of my eyes. "From my father's purse." The vein in his neck bulged.

"Sir Stapleford gave it to me."

"The girl tells nothing but lies!" shouted Mrs Wilson triumphantly.

"But you were there!" I cried.

"I reckon as to how she is the murderer, Sir. It makes sense. Some kind of Bolshie I reckon," opined the policeman.

"I only found the body," I said as calmly as I could. "Please ask Sir Stapleford about the coin. He will tell you he gave it to me himself."

"As if you don't know," sneered the Constable, "Sir Stapleford is dead. Murdered."

A Lady of Ill Repute

With what my mother would have denounced as an unfortunate tendency towards the melodramatic I fainted quite away at the word murder.

The next thing I knew I was back in that wretched library. I had been lain on a rather hard settle. As I came drowsily around I realised Mr Richard was talking.

"It's a damn rotten thing to happen to one's Papa, but on a national level it's a tragedy. Papa was the back-up man for George. The party's lost two of its best men in quick succession."

"Party, Sir?" It was a man's voice I did not recognise. Well spoken, but with the sense that every vowel was earned and with a faint twang of an accent that could not quite be diminished. I guessed this must be the Inspector.

"Unionists, man! The Unionists! We've finally got a shot to unseat the Liberals."

"Ah, party politics. Not something the force is connected with, Sir."

"Yes, but surely, you must see," blustered Mr Richard, "this could be a politically motivated crime. Someone trying to bring down the country!"

"Correct me if I'm wrong here, Sir, but it's you Unionists that want to turn the government out of power."

I stifled a giggle. The man had it right.

"Good God man! We want a better run country, not to bring it to its knees!"

"I see your point, Sir. Now, if I'm not mistaken that young girl is awake."

Mr Richard pointed an accusatory finger at me in a manner that even I feel a neutral critic would have found even more melodramatic than my fainting fit. "You! You girl! You're Bolshevik, aren't you? A Marxist."

I sat up. My head thumped unpleasantly. "I am not entirely sure one can be both," I said.

"Ha!" Mr Richard thumped a fist into the palm of his hand. "There you have it. No serving maid knows anything of politics! She's an impostor."

The Inspector, a small neat man in a discreet woolen suit and carefully combed short beard, regarded me from small brown eyes. I shifted uncomfortably. It was not that I found his manner exactly threatening, but I had the sense of a keen brain working behind a perfect mask. Also, while I was not guilty of murder, I was guilty of deception and duplicity which does not fit well with a lifelong career as a vicar's daughter.

"Well, girl, what do you know of politics?"

"I cannot say I think of it often, Sir. It has little to do with me."

The Inspector smiled thinly. "I wish all women felt that way."

I bridled and suppressed an urge to confess a sudden conversion to suffragettism.

"You have no knowledge of the Bolshevik philosophy?"

"Very little."

"But some?" Mr Richard pounced like a cat on a mouse. Fortunately, it was only a verbal pounce.

"Only what I have seen in the papers, Sir."

"Sir Stapleford," began the Inspector.

"What?"

"It is a hereditary title, is it not, Sir? I have that right?"

Mr Richard sat down heavily on a chair and rubbed his brow with one large hand. "Yes. Yes. Feels strange to hear it. Makes the poor old Pater's death more real."

"I am sorry, Sir. I was going to explain that

I think it is unlikely that a girl of a build such as your servant here could have overpowered Sir Stapleford."

"Then she is an accomplice!"

"If you will permit me, Sir, I have been making some enquiries of my own." He raised his voice. "Constable, send him in!"

The door opened and the man who had trodden on Siegfried's tail came in. My heart sank.

"Could you confirm this young woman was the one you saw in the snug of the Red Lion."

The man glowered at me. "It was."

"When was this?" asked the Inspector.

"Be about four of the clock I reckon."

"You see, Sir Stapleford, unless this girl can fly it would be impossible for her to be your father's assailant."

"She could still be an accomplice. I know there is something wrong about her. Doubtless her partner in crime has fled. Probably half way back to Russia by now. She was the one who gave him the knowledge he needed of the house. That's how these damn Bolsheviks work. Infiltration."

"Was she with someone?"

"Aye," answered the man. My heart stopped as I waited to see what he said next. "But I didnae see his face. It were too dark. I only saw her cos I trod on her great lump of . . ."

"You were very rude and threatening," I

jumped in before he could reveal the presence of a large white wolfhound of which I doubted there were many in the neighborhood. "It is my belief you were intoxicated and were not seeing straight!"

"Why you little bitch . . ."

"That's enough!" commanded the Police Inspector.

"But she's taking my good name!" protested the large man.

"You should have thought of that before you chose to enter a tavern in the afternoon. Go now before I start asking questions."

The man threw me an evil look and left, muttering. I breathed a sigh of relief.

"There's no need for you to be looking so smug, Missy," said the Inspector. "I advise you now to tell the whole truth and reveal the name of your companion."

My position was an impossible one. "I prefer not to say."

"Young lady, I warn you, keeping important information from the police is a jailable offence. What was the name of your companion?"

He fairly shouted the last few words at me and I think it was this above all else that decided me not to say. I had no idea if Mr Bertram would even own up to our association and if he denied it, well, things would only get worse. I kept my lips together and cast my eyes down. The Inspector walked over to the door and yanked it open. "Get that housekeeper in here."

I sat silently, hoping for a rescue that never came. How could it be that I had no one to take me away from all this?

Mrs Wilson swept into the room. Her eyes alighted on me and her lips curled. "How can I be of service, Sirs?" Her voice was demure and soft, but I could see the triumph implicit in every inch of her frame.

"What can you tell me of the character of this woman?" asked the Inspector.

"I am afraid, Sir, the fault is mine. I was prevailed upon to engage her services for a fortnight trial period without references."

"Without references? Is that not unusual?"

I saw Mrs Wilson shoot a fleeting glance in the new Sir Stapleford's direction. I was not sure if the Inspector noticed. After a moment's hesitation, she said simply, "We are quite remote in the country, Sir, and few young girls, unless they are born local, are interested in working here. They prefer to be in London."

"So you have no knowledge of this young woman's character?"

"Only what I have observed, Inspector, and that is not good."

"Explain yourself," said the Inspector. "I

want detail, not conjecture."

"It appears she did indeed gain the coin from the late Sir Stapleford, but I could not say how it was acquired."

"Wilson!" barked Mr Richard. "The man is not yet in his grave."

A faint blush flitted under the bone white skin. "I meant only, Sir, that this young woman was clearly intent on ingratiating herself with her betters."

"Is that not a proper thing for a servant to do?" asked the Inspector. "Or are you suggesting something more?"

"In my experience, a maid servant is eager to please her betters, but she is also keen to remain unobserved. In fact, she should display a deference and an awareness of her station that would cause any actual interaction with her master to be an overwhelming ordeal she would prefer to avoid. In Euphemia's case, she appears to court the attention of her betters. I had information from our butler, Mr Holdsworth, that she was even seen to accost Mr Richard in the scullery room!"

"One might wonder what Mr Richard was doing in the scullery room," I murmured under my breath.

"What you are saying, Mrs Wilson, is this young woman displays no understanding of her place. Would you go as far as to say she shows contempt for our class structure?"

"Yes," said Mrs Wilson vehemently. "I would say so, Sir."

The Inspector rounded on me. "It appears then I must revise my initial impression of you, young woman. Are you a Bolshevik?"

"No, of course not," I could not keep the scorn out of my voice.

"Or a Marxist?"

"She's hardly going to admit it, is she Inspector?" said Sir Richard.

"You'd be surprised what criminals will admit to under the stern eye of the law, Sir."

"I had nothing to do with Sir Stapleford's death and I have no interest in politics," I announced loudly.

"We'll see if a night in jail changes your mind," said the Inspector. "Constable, in here!"

"What!" I cried, jumping to my feet. "You can't throw me in jail. I haven't done anything."

"You have refused to answer police questions. That's enough for me! Constable, I say!"

The door opened. For a moment I considered diving out of the window, but it was closed and we were on the first floor. Besides, I would have to get past the gauntlet of Wilson and Sir Richard. I thought about screaming, but beyond resulting in my own exhaustion and sore throat I could not see what it could achieve. I was trapped.

Mr Bertram came through the open door. "Richard," he appealed, ignoring everyone else in the room, "is it true? Has Papa been found dead?"

Sir Richard came forward and placed a hand on his half-brother's shoulder. "I'm afraid so, Bertie. Looks like the same bloke that did for Cousin Georgie came back for the Pater."

Mr Bertram looked at him with blank, empty eyes. He shook off his brother's arm. "But that makes no sense."

"I know it's a shock, old boy, but we think it's a Bolshevik plot. Two good men of the party practically on the eve of the election."

Mr Bertram shook his head. "I don't know, Dickie. Why here? Why us?"

"Ask her, Sir!" spat Mrs Wilson. "Ask the little Bolshie yourself."

"What?" asked Mr Bertram, dazed. He seemed to finally realise the room was full of people. He addressed the Inspector. "What do they mean? What do you know?"

The Inspector coughed. "It has been suggested, Sir, that this young woman might have political leanings."

Mr Bertram blinked. The Inspector placed a finger under his collar and pulled as if it had suddenly become too tight "Are you mad, man?" asked Mr Bertram.

"There is some circumstantial evidence against her, Sir. These Bolshies they're – excusing your pardon Mrs Wilson – damned clever. A night in the jail will loosen her tongue."

"How many have you met?" asked Mr Bertram.

"Well, I haven't exactly met any, Sir," said the Inspector, his accent slipping under pressure. "But I've been briefed. All the force has. Serious times and all that. I can't say more."

"Good God!" bellowed Mr Bertram. "I've never heard such arrant nonsense. It's my father who is dead. If anyone has cause to look for the guilty it is I, but throwing blame left and right will not help bring his killer to justice!"

"She wouldn't answer my questions, Sir. You heard her, Sir Stapleford. She wouldn't."

Mr Bertram blanched at the use of his father's title towards his brother. Mr Richard clapped a brotherly hand on his shoulder.

"It's true, Bertie. I know the girl is something of a prodigy for you, but she was seen consorting with some suspicious character in the Red Lion this afternoon and she won't give his name."

"Is that all!" exclaimed Mr Bertram, shaking off the hand impatiently. "There's a perfectly obvious explanation . . ."

His eyes met mine and he hesitated.

"And that would be, Sir?" asked the

Inspector.

Mr Bertram took a deep breath and tore his eyes away from mine. "I am sure my brother has told you of the suspicions we had when she arrived at the house."

"Suspicions?" cried the Inspector.

Mr Bertram waved his hand dismissively. "Nothing political. A young woman, obviously educated above her station, without visible means and," he lowered his voice and leant in towards the Inspector, but I could still hear him add, "and not unattractive."

"You mean?" asked the Inspector and I was sure he had little more idea than I did what Mr Bertram meant.

"Come now, Inspector. We're both men of the world. I am sure I do not need to spell this out. I will only say that to such a one a local tavern must have been a great temptation."

I had absolutely no idea what he was talking about, but I was certain if I did I would not be pleased. But then whatever he was suggesting, he was my only ally. I had the sense to keep my tongue between my teeth. I had no desire to discover the comforts of the local jail.

"I see," said the Inspector slowly. "You mean?"

"Exactly," said Mr Bertram. "I have an idea, but no I do not want to trespass on your territory."

"I like to consider myself an open-minded man, Sir," said the Inspector. He remained neat and composed. There was no more collar tugging, but I thought I saw something resembling panic behind his eyes. Here was a man very much in awe of his betters. If only he knew what kind of people were before him!

"My sister, Richenda, has had some success with young women."

"Sir?"

"She runs, or is an advocate, for a centre in the city. She has, I believe, already taken a liking to Euphemia. Perhaps if the girl came to trust her she might be prepared to be more open with you."

The Inspector bridled. "Indeed, Sir! This young miss is required by law to answer my questions."

"And I am sure she would if you had not been so austere, Inspector. You must know that women in her position are notoriously wary of the law of which you are such a formidable specimen."

I choked on a giggle and tried to look contrite. Mr Bertram flicked me a glance. "You see how discomposed your presence makes her? I have no doubt she has no direct involvement in this situation, for all her pretty words she is a woman and her intellect is naturally limited."

A retort flashed to my mind, but Mr Bertram caught my eye and I kept my mouth shut.

"Well, I don't know, Sir. It is most irregular."

"C'mon Bertie, let the man do his job! A night in the jail will do the girl no harm."

"Indeed, Sir," piped up Mrs Wilson, "it is the only possible course of sensible action."

Unexpectedly, the Inspector took offence. "Is it indeed, Ma'am? I'll ask you not to trouble yourself to do my job, Mrs Wilson. If you've no objection, I think I'd like to go along with Mr Stapleford's plan!"

Sir Richard shrugged. "As you wish. I would not want to interfere in a judicial process." He gave Mr Bertram a cool look. "What is your plan, Bertie?"

Mr Bertram did not flinch. "I suggest she is given into my sister's custody in the function of lady's maid. Richenda is currently without one and this girl's background makes her suitably knowledgeable about such fripperies. It may be that my sister is able to gain her confidence and glean information from her such as she may not even know she has."

"As she may not even know she has, Sir?" enquired the baffled policeman.

"Exactly, Inspector."

"Well . . ."

"What harm could it do and it might help a lot," said Mr Bertram mysteriously.

"Euphemia, return to the linen room. There are some sheets that need mending," commanded Mrs Wilson. "The gentlemen can more properly discuss your fate without you present." She turned to the Inspector. "If your man would care to take a cup of tea in the kitchen, he can keep an eye on her and ensure she does not run."

"A very good idea, Mrs Wilson. I almost envy the man."

"I'll escort her down and arrange for refreshments to be sent up, Inspector."

She hustled me out of the room. I had no doubt she would quickly return and argue against me. I would have to trust Mr Bertram. When we reached the linen room she opened the door and fairly pushed me inside. I stumbled forward. The door slammed behind me and to my utter amazement I heard the sound of a key turning in the lock.

To my shame, my immediate reaction was to bang loudly on the door and shout. No one came to my rescue and although later I thought I could discern the sounds of movement within the kitchen, not even the kind Mrs Deighton, it appeared, was prepared to release me from my prison. The room was ill lit and smelled of damp I was overcome by the uncharitable thought that I hoped every single fresh bed ever made up in this house would always be uncomfortably moist.

The devil may make work for idle hands, but industry stills the demons within. By the time I was released, I had repaired six sheets and re-sewn one that had the appearance of having been repaired by someone limited by ham-fisted trotters instead of fingers.

It was Merry who freed me. If she had found me on the base of her shoe she could not have looked more disdainful. "To think I was taken in by the likes of you," she spat. "You, lording it over me when I was breaking my heart over Mr Georgie."

She turned her back and walked off. I emerged blinking in the corridor. "Merry!" I called after her. "Merry!"

There were good reasons for everyone to be in the kitchen, but it felt like they were waiting for me. Mr Holdsworth was frowning over the silver. Mrs Deighton was stirring a pot vigorously enough to splatter her apron and muttering to herself. Merry was setting out the dishes for serving in a manner I can only describe as aggressive and Mrs Wilson stood, obelisk like in the corner, smugly surveying the scene.

"I don't understand," I blurted out.

"What's there to understand?" demanded Merry, smashing down an earthenware dish hard on the well-scrubbed wooden table. "You're to wait on Miss Richenda. Maybe she'll take you when she leaves. She's experience of your sort. Good riddance. That's what I say."

"My sort?" I said blankly.

Mr Holdsworth paused in his polishing. "Mrs Wilson was kind enough to furnish us with the explanation Mr Bertram gave of your actions."

"Really," I said in what I hoped were freezing accents. "Would you care to explain it to me, Mrs Wilson. I confess I did not quite follow that part of the conversation."

Mrs Wilson sneered at me. It was her usual expression, but she managed to deepen it for me. "Oh, I think you understood all too well. I think you can put two and two together if I inform you Miss Richenda supports a charity that runs a shelter for fallen women."

"What!" I shrieked.

"And you going on about Mr Georgie's dishonourable intentions," added Merry.

"Oh be quiet, Merry. A leopard does not change its spots," snapped Mrs Wilson.

"Am I to understand that Mr Bertram has let it be known to staff and family that I am a fallen woman?" For once, I took no pains to modify my accent. I must have made an impression, because even Mrs Wilson seemed somewhat taken aback.

"Do you dispute it?" she enquired icily.

"I most certainly do," I cried. "And I will not stay a moment longer in this house."

I did not wait to see what effect my declaration had, but flung out of the room with as much dignity as the granddaughter of an Earl wearing a maid's uniform can muster.

I found the Inspector in the upstairs hall. He was standing by the fire, staring down into an open notebook in his hand. "Am I a suspect?" I demanded.

He looked up in surprise. "Everyone is a suspect." I am sure he almost added "ma'am"! I was, after all, still very cross and at my most impressive.

"If I furnish you with my direction do you have any legal objection to my quitting this dreadful house?"

"Well no, but . . ."

I did not wait to hear the rest, but stormed off in the direction of my room.

I hate packing. It is a tedious and depressing task, but when one is very angry it can be quite satisfying to bang about and dismantle a room. It was because of this manner of completing my task that I did not realise I had been joined in the room until a hand was placed upon my shoulder. I whirled round and looked directly into the face of the new Sir Stapleford.

"Sir!" I cried in an outrageous accent.

"Leaving us, Euphemia?" he said leaning his face close to mine. I could not help but notice his ginger moustache was twitching like a caterpillar. It was fascinating in the worst way. "I think you are making the right decision. A girl such as you is wasted as a maid."

I attempted to put some distance between us, but the room was very small.

"I will be running for Parliament now, in my father's place," he continued. "It is considered a safe seat. I will win. Then . . ." and he took a pace towards me, "I will be spending a lot of time in London. A lot of time on my own. I shall need a companion." He drew his eyebrows down and looked at me from beneath them. "You understand what I mean, Euphemia?"

I nodded. It was the wrong thing to do. His face relaxed and he smiled. "Now Pater is dead, I shall be a rich man. A very rich man. I shall have the kind of wealth that knocks Bertie's little inheritance into a cocked hat. My companion would have everything her heart desired. Do you understand?"

I nodded again. His large frame stood between me and the door.

He sat down on my bed and patted the place beside him. "So it is agreed we are to be friends?"

What else could I do but pretend. I nodded.

I attempted to slip past him with the pretence of sitting on the other side, the side nearest the door, but he caught my wrist and pulled me down beside him.

"I feel I should ask, not that it makes any real difference now, but did you know my Cousin George before you worked here? Perhaps in London?"

I found my voice. It sounded very small. "No, Sir, I did not."

He smiled and caressed my palm with his fingertips. I tried not to be sick. He still had my wrist in a tight grasp. I was overly aware of the strength that lingered beneath his fleshy frame. "It is no matter. But I am relieved. It would have been much worse when you discovered the body if you had known him."

I swallowed and nodded again.

"It must have been an awful experience?"

I nodded again.

"I don't suppose you noticed anything? Something you might not have mentioned to the police?" he softened his voice. "Something that is preying on your mind? You can tell me, Euphemia. Now we are friends. I will be looking after you. You can tell me anything. Anything you might have found. It would be easier this way, much easier."

I had the strong impression things would

go better for me if I had something to tell him. Unfortunately, I did not have the faintest idea what he was talking about.

"No, Sir. I'm sorry."

The fingers tightened painfully about my wrist. "Think, girl! Things can go well between us or they can go very badly. The choice is yours."

He pulled me roughly towards him. That horrendous ginger caterpillar bore down towards my face. He was about to kiss me. I opened my mouth and screamed.

A Respectable Gentleman

My courage failed me and I closed my eyes. I readied my knee for the most unladylike of actions, when there was a knock on the door. Sir Richard sprang away from me as if I was a rare contagion. The Butler's calm voice reached us. "Euphemia, I've arranged for the carrier to come and collect you tomorrow evening. If you could come down now and give directions to his boy it would be most helpful."

"Of course. I will come at once." I almost shouted with relief. I pushed roughly past my tormentor, opened the door and fairly fell into Mr Holdsworth's arms.

He very properly set me back on my heels. He did not say a word, but began to walk quickly away. I had a strong impulse to burst into tears.

I ran after him. "You must not believe what they are saying of me," I protested.

"I am given to understand you are no longer a member of our staff and as such your actions and morals are no concern of mine."

"But it isn't true," I cried. "None of it."

"I hope I am incorrect, but it seemed to me as if you were not alone in your room."

"That wasn't my fault! I never sought his attentions."

"That I can believe." The Butler stopped at the top of the servants' stairs. "Dinner is over and I have further duties to attend to."

"The carrier's boy? Is he in the kitchen?"

"Neither the carrier nor his boy came today."

I looked directly into his eyes. "I see."

The Butler nodded and headed off down the stairs. I followed once more, but more slowly. I had little idea of where to go, but I was afraid Sir Richard was still waiting for me in my room. His absence would eventually be noticed, so I was hopeful of being able to return later, but where for now? I had no desire to be caught alone, but neither had I any desire to meet any of the inmates of this house, above or below stairs. I had never felt so despised.

I reached the first floor landing and without thinking found my feet turning towards the library. I slipped quietly into the servants' passage and made my way to the secret door. I do not know what I expected to find. The passageway was ill lit, but in my heart I knew all my misfortune in this house stemmed from the murder I had been unfortunate enough to stumble across. Perhaps, if a solution was found, my name could be cleared?

I leant against the secret panel gently. It gave in with a soft click. A stream of buttery light cut across the passageway floor. On the other side I could hear someone pacing. I pressed my eye to the crack and saw the figure of Mr Bertram. He had a glass of brandy in one hand and the other was holding a half-smoked cigar.

I do not know what came over me, but my heart, which has always been the most reliable of organs for pumping blood around my body all at once, switched to providing me with raw, fiery anger. I plunged through the door, not even thinking to care if he was alone.

"How could you do that to me? How could you blacken my virtue? You've cost me my position. You may have even cost my family their home. And for what? So no scandal attaches to your pure white family, because if that's what you're trying to do I have information for you. This precious family of yours is riddled with deception, vanity and sin!"

Mr Bertram, who had startled somewhat at

my entrance, waited for me to draw breath. Then he said simply, "I know."

Feeling as if all the wind had been sucked from my sails, I sank down onto the settle, dropped my head in my hands and to my horror began to weep. Mr Bertram, like most gentlemen with a tearful woman, was immediately at a loss.

"Euphemia! No. Please don't Euphemia. I was only trying to protect you!"

This appalling untruth stopped my tears as swiftly as if a valve had been shut off. "How dare you! How dare you say such a thing!"

At this Mr Bertram threw himself down onto his knees and grasped both my hands in his. "It's the truth, Euphemia. I swear."

For one heady moment I felt myself the heroine of some fantastical adventure. My heart lurched within my breast as I waited for Mr Bertram's next inevitable words.

"I think Richard killed them both."

Whatever I had thought he might have uttered at this juncture, this was certainly not it. I snatched my hands from him and broke away. In my best Sunday voice I said, "I think you should rise, Mr Bertram. You look most ridiculous."

"This is not the reaction I expected, Euphemia," he retorted, levering himself to his feet.

"I think, Sir," I responded, still breathing

hard, "that we both find ourselves somewhat at a disadvantage."

"You really aren't what one would expect in a maid, Euphemia."

"You were about to tell me about your brother?"

"I'm pretty certain that Richard had made some bad investments. My father had not only cut off his personal allowance, but was speaking of disinheriting him."

"But to kill your own father!"

"I know," said Mr Bertram, seating himself on the settle. "It's so impossible, but . . ."

"But?"

Mr Bertram sighed. "Are you aware of the family business?"

I shook my head.

"Father has a small bank, but the greater part of our fortune comes from arms trading."

I digested this for a moment. "This is what that journalist meant when he said you traded in death."

"I'm afraid so. I don't personally work in the business. Father allowed this because I have issues with my heart. He preferred to let people think it is my physical infirmity rather than my strength of conscience that inclines me not to work with him."

"Which is it?"

"I cannot wholly claim it is my conscience. While I have inherited an independence from my late godfather, I still live under my father's roof and eat at his table. All my life I have helped spend his blood money."

I felt the unaccountable need to place more distance between us and moved from the settle to a nearby chair. For a servant to sit in her master's presence is not acceptable, but I felt we were moving without the bounds of the normal servile relationship. Besides, I had every intention of quitting this day.

"I do not think your actions as a child can be held to account. We do not choose our parents."

He nodded. "But it changes you. Knowing your father is a party to murder on an horrific scale. If you knew one tenth of what is happening in Africa. I am only glad you do not."

"One could argue that it is not the weapon, but how it is used."

"It's a weak argument at best," said Mr Bertram. "My family have been instrumental in the development of some of the most terrible of weapons. And we choose who we sell them to. Now, more than ever, we are shaping the future of the world."

"I know very little about politics."

But Mr Bertram was no longer listening to me. It was as if a flood-gate had opened within him. "Richard over indulged one night. He was boasting of what he and my cousin were doing. If he hadn't been under the influence he would never have told me, but it made him less than coherent. I knew their mother was vaguely related to the Schnieders – despite the name it's a French company. There's a new field gun, a vile thing that can mow men down like wheat before a scythe, and this company are planning on selling it to both the French and the Germans. The French are still bogged down in the Wadai war, but it's more than that. They're investing for the future. There are rumours of heavy artillery tractors. That would be an inhuman abomination. It would change warfare forever. Of course, everyone is saying it is all in aid of the defence of the Trans-Sahara trade routes, but I don't believe it. I have nightmares of where the world is going – where it is going, steered by those such as my father and brother. Our money is made from blood and we spend it to shed more."

"It might be vile, but of itself it is hardly illegal nor a motive for murder," I interjected.

"Euphemia, many people, important people, believe war with Germany is coming. If it happens it will make the Boer Wars look like a brawl in a public house; the Wadai war a mere inconvenience. Russia is in chaos. We assume the French will stand as our friends, but . . . but . . .

some of the men in the party favour Germany. Richard favours Germany. He told me that night it is because of his influence that the same technology is being offered to the Germans."

"Men often say things when drunk that are a little over large, do they not?"

"You don't understand. I come from a family of monsters. They are capable of anything."

Mr Bertram's exposition was arousing a number of conflicting circumstances in my breast. At the best of times these would have been difficult to deal with, but in this moment, in this conundrum of class differential that I had willingly entered upon and was now attempting to extricate myself from, I no longer knew which way was up and which was down. I was overwhelmingly aware of the man's passion and his desire to do right. That he might know more than me about the state of the world was easy to accept. That the state of world affairs were relevant to these two murders, less so. I did the only thing I could do. I doused his ardour with common sense.

"There may be something in what you think, Sir. But aside from the deaths of these two men, the only circumstances of note I observe are that someone has broken into my room and that your brother's reaction to me varies alarmingly for no cause I can suppose."

"You are moderately attractive and a maid in

his father's house. Trust me, that is enough for Richard."

I bridled instinctively. I doubt anyone is at their best in a maid's uniform with their hair suitably braided, but moderately attractive? It was little better than being compared to a kitchen cat.

"I meant you *need* be no more than moderately attractive," added Mr Bertram lamely.

I blushed. It was inappropriate for me either as a maid or as the granddaughter of an Earl to seek compliments. "If you will recall," I said sharply, "your brother had more than ample occasion to observe me prior to suddenly finding me an object worthy of his attention."

Mr Bertram cocked his head on one side, rather like a raven surveying a worm. "You are implying some specific action caused his change in behaviour."

"I assure you it was nothing I did!"

Mr Bertram shook his head. "No, I was not suggesting that. You have more than enough sense to see my brother for what he is."

"And more to the point a strict moral code!"

"Yes. Yes, Euphemia. But I think you've hit on something here. Obviously it was after Cousin George's murder, but before my father's?"

"He tried to sneak a kiss from me in the pantry before your father's murder. Afterwards he was, as you saw, keen to have me thrown from the house. But not one hour since he offered me the opportunity to become his close female companion."

"Good God!" cried Bertram, rising to his feet in indignation.

"I declined, of course, and this is what has reinforced my desire to leave your house."

"But you must not! You and I are the only ones who have some sense of this business. Neither man who died was of an estimable character, but this does not justify their killing! I thought you agreed this?"

I sighed. "I do. But my position is extremely difficult."

"What did Richard say to you?"

"He offered for me to become his companion."

"I did understand that part. Did he say anything else?"

I thought for a moment. "He did ask me if I had known your cousin before."

"He thinks you know something."

"Or I have something?" I countered.

"You were the first person to come across George. Did you check his pockets?"

"It didn't occur to me at the time."

"That's a pity," said Bertram, sitting again.

"I can assure you, Sir, the next time I come

across an unfortunate murdered relative of yours I will not only search his pockets, but make a quick sketch of the scene."

Mr Bertram smiled. "Don't be cross, Euphemia. I'm only trying to make sense of this. I quite understand why you would want to leave this house, but if Richard, or anyone else, thinks you have something or know something that might help catch the killer, you may not complete your journey home."

A sensation of icy coldness washed over me as I acknowledged the truth of his words. "But I don't know anything," I said weakly. Suddenly, Mr Bertram was at my side. "I did not mean to alarm you."

I looked up at him. "I can't see how anyone can think I know anything. It was dark in the corridor and your cousin was very dead. There were no last words. There was no one else there."

"Then it must be thought that you found something. Richard must think you have something."

"If you imagine in all this that Richard did murder your father, then his primary motive was to not be discovered in some shady business deal that involves the armament industry."

Mr Bertram nodded.

"If you are right, your brother cannot possibly have murdered your cousin."

"How do you deduce that?"

"If you are right, the only possible explanation for Mr Richard's behaviour is that he fears blackmail. You are right he must believe I found something on your cousin's body or perhaps I was even involved in a blackmail attempt that went wrong. He may believe I turned up at this house prearranged to meet Cousin George and extort money. That I have acted in a manner unlike that of a normal maid will not have helped my case."

"My dear, you hardly behave like a woman," chuckled Mr Bertram. He flinched under the look this comment occasioned and added, "I meant only that you display not only a code of honour, but the ability to use logic. Neither of which are customarily regarded as attributes of your sex."

I smiled slightly at that. "I am a great trial to my mother."

"Who is she?"

I shook my head. "It doesn't matter. I think you are right. I think George was being blackmailed and that it concerned some business dealing that he was involved in with Richard. I am very much afraid that Richard panicked and took your father's life."

"You may be giving Richard credit for emotions he does not possess. I think he saw an opportunity to pass off a murder. The Inspector still favours the Bolsheviks, you know. My father's death has assured his secret, given him a place in the Commons where he will be able to use his influence to line his pockets and of course, avoid my father disinheriting him."

"But this would mean he did not kill your cousin."

"No," Mr Bertram paused. "It also means it is not safe for you to leave this house."

"I could mention that people do seem to die here with alarming regularity."

"I know. But you have a greater chance of safety if you stay in sight of others than if you are alone wandering through the countryside on your way home."

"I would be with a carrier."

"Would you trust he had not been bought?"

"Mr Bertram, you are becoming ridiculous! This is not some international conspiracy!"

"Maybe not, but I would not be surprised if a carrier could be bribed to drop you in the middle of the countryside. He might even be told it was a romantic rendezvous."

"You do have a devious mind, Sir."

"Thank you."

"But what is to be done? We do not know enough to approach the Police Inspector. To be frank, I would prefer not to draw further attention to myself unless we had some definite evidence."

"I think you are right, Euphemia. He may still reckon you as the Russian revolutionary intent on taking down our bourgeois lifestyle." He paused a moment. "The family lawyer will be attending shortly to start the process of winding up my father's affairs. I don't think we can wait. I think you, and perhaps others, stand in considerable danger until this knot can be untangled. I will go immediately to London to see him. I am my father's executor, not Richard, so he can hardly object if I look over the accounts. I will also make discreet enquiries into any business deals that may have been made between Richard and George."

My dismay must have shown on my face.

"I will only be gone for two days at the most. You are right, we need evidence."

"What if we are wrong?" I asked quietly.

"Then we will have to think again. No harm will have been done. I will not voice our suspicions until we know everything."

I nodded. It was a good plan. "We cannot be sure your brother murdered your father, but if he did then there could be two murderers in this house."

"You must take great care."

I lifted my chin. "I will avoid being alone with anyone. That strikes me as the best precaution."

"I thought . . ."

The door opened behind us. "Really, everything is getting very lax. You'd think with two murders in the house, Holdsworth would appreciate the necessity of cocktails."

"Honestly, Richenda, you're a callous girl." It was Mr Richard and his twin. A thunderstruck look crossed his face as he saw Mr Bertram and I, chairs close, and obviously in deep and intimate conversation. "Good God!"

Mr Bertram rose. "I would have preferred to have communicated this to you privately, Richard, but Miss St John and I have an understanding."

Miss Richenda screeched, "You cannot marry the maid, Bertie!"

Mr Richard nudged her with his elbow. "I don't think he is referring to marriage, Sister. Perhaps you had better leave, so we can settle this like gentlemen."

Miss Richenda turned to go, then hesitated and walked back into the room. "Euphemia, is this what you want?"

"No," I cried, finally finding my voice. Her question released my tongue which had been struck dumb with surprise. "Of course, it isn't. I don't want to belong to any man!"

Miss Richenda nodded. "Quite right," she said. "You had better come and work for me."

Onions and Elections

The doorbell rang loud and insistent. I ignored it. Mr Holdsworth passed through the kitchen, his face creased in a frown and sweat upon his brow.

"Mercy!" cried Merry, "that must be the thousandth time that bell has rung this morning."

"I hope not," commented Mrs Deighton from among her pots on the range. "I'm cooking for thirty, not a thousand. The potatoes would never go round."

Merry laughed gaily. I sat as quietly as I could and attempted to fade into the background. I carefully shaved the skin from yet another carrot and wondered why on earth I had imagined that Richenda's generous impulse would be more than that. At Mrs Wilson's suggestion that I might be of more use in the kitchen on the night of the big dinner, Miss Richenda had handed me over without a backward glance.

Mrs Wilson came into the kitchen and, despite my best efforts, noticed me. "Ah, Euphemia. I have left you a little present in the scullery." I looked at her blankly. Mrs Wilson clapped her hands. "Chop! Chop! Cook needs this done as quickly as possible." She came over to my bowl. "Goodness gracious! Mrs Deighton, did you not keep an eye on this girl? These carrots really will not do. Merry, you'll have to prepare another batch."

Merry gave me a filthy look. "But I'm already doing the pastry, Mrs Wilson, and it's not my job."

"Need I remind you, young woman, that tonight is the Election dinner. By midnight tonight we should have a Member in the family again."

"Member?" queried Merry.

"Member of Parliament!"

"There is no doubt Mr Richard will win?" I asked.

Mrs Wilson's beady black eyes homed in on me. "Of course not. Whatever your personal ideals, girl, this is a safe Conservative seat."

Several retorts sprang to my tongue, but I pressed my lips tight shut. I doubted Mrs Wilson had ever bothered to form an opinion through thought, but had acquired what little veneer of understanding she had through contact with the family. Much like a vegetable will acquire mould.

"I am going to my room for tea!" said Mrs Wilson. Merry and Mrs Deighton exchanged a look I could not fathom. "Kindly clean out the old kitchen grate, Euphemia. Someone has burnt something in it."

"Isn't that what grates are for?" I muttered as Mrs Wilson paraded out of the room, for all the world as if her skirts were made of peacock feathers rather than plain, black silk.

"That's a right odd thing," commented Mrs Deighton. "I noticed it earlier, but with all the comings and goings on it quite slipped my mind. Brush is in the linen room, Euphemia."

Confused, I made for the room with the sheets where I'd been so recently imprisoned. Merry bustled up beside me. "Not there. That's the still room." I must have looked completely bemused for she giggled almost in her old friendly manner. "Wilson calls the rooms after what they were first used for. Says it's tradition."

"It's confusing."

"Never mind. I shouldn't think you'll be around long enough to let it bother you," snapped Merry. "I hear how it's Mr Bertram who you're making up to now."

"It was always Mr Bertram," I protested. "No, I don't mean that. I mean the only rumours about me were about him. And they're not true anyway."

Merry shrugged. I sighed, picked up the brush and pan and took them over to the grate. Someone had indeed started a small fire in the centre. There was a small sooty mound among the gleaming metal. Clearly, since the arrival of the range, this grate and been nothing more than ornamental. How foolish to burn something here if you wanted to hide its presence. But then there didn't need to be anything nefarious about this, did there?

Except that there was a small curl of white amongst the darkness. I bent down and pulled a scrap of paper from the soot. It was a single line from a letter. Written in a well-practised spidery hand were the words *Lucy is carrying your child.* I rocked back on my heels. Who was Lucy? Mrs Deighton turned from her pots to the salt crock and without thinking I slipped the paper into my pocket. I brushed the grate quickly and emptied the soot into the waste area outside.

After the warmth of the kitchen, entering the garden was like plunging into a frozen lake. The cold air pinched at my cheeks, but no clarity came with the chill. I darted back inside, returned the brush to its quarters and slipped into the scullery to see what Mrs Wilson's "little present" was. It turned out to be a truly enormous pile of onions. Tears streamed down my face as I peeled and chopped them, but I barely noticed them as my mind raced. Something told me this burnt letter was at the heart of everything that had happened. It had to be. One did not find mysterious, portentously worded scored missives without them being vitally important. Surely fate was not cruel enough to make this unimportant? I finally had the key to everything and I didn't understand it. I needed to talk to someone, but who could I trust?

When the last onion was chopped, I braved the garden again to throw the peelings onto the compost pile. As I came back in, I made a decision. I placed my bucket by the door and stole up the servants' stairs into the house.

I tried the library first, but it was empty. Reluctantly, and knowing this would not enhance my reputation if I was caught, I made my way towards Mr Bertram's bedchamber. I knocked softly on the door, and not wishing to be observed in the corridor, slipped inside at once. The room was empty. The bed pristine and unslept in. Gone were the trinkets from the dressing table. With a sinking heart I realised that Mr Bertram must still be in London.

I was making my way dejectedly down the

servants' stairs when Merry bounded up to meet me. "There you are!" she exclaimed. "I don't know why he thinks you can help, but Mr Holdsworth is asking for you. You're to come at once."

I nodded and followed her down.

"Don't you want to know why Mr Holdsworth wants yer?" asked Merry.

"I expect he'll tell me," I said distractedly.

"You are a strange fish," Merry said without rancour. "Most maids would be terrified that they were going to be sacked."

I shrugged. "I'm sure Mrs Wilson would never delegate that pleasure to someone else."

"It's more likely to be her out on her ear," said Merry darkly. "It was all very well when Sir Stapleford was alive – the old Sir Stapleford. He had a soft spot for the old cow, but I don't see Mr Richard cutting her any slack."

"Sir Stapleford had a soft spot for Mrs Wilson?" I repeated, amazed.

"Yeah, there's always been whispers that they 'ad a past – if you know what I means. Never could quite bring myself to believe it. Though I don't suppose she was born a dried-up old prune."

I shook my head, trying to gather my thoughts. "What has Mrs Wilson done? Why does she need to be cut slack?"

"She's gone for a cup of tea. And you know what that means."

I stopped a step behind Merry and looked down on her. "No, I don't."

"A cup of tea," said Merry stressing each word unnecessarily. She sighed. "She's gone on the bottle."

"She's a drunkard?" I gasped.

"On and off. Always been a bit of a problem for her. Normally she makes sure it doesn't get in the way of the running of the house, but what with the old master getting killed she gone off her 'ead a bit if you asks me."

"Did she ever have any children?"

Merry laughed out loud. "Gor, you do ask some stupid things. Cos not. I reckon how she's never . . . you know."

"But I thought you said Sir Stapleford and her . . ."

"I never said any such thing," snapped Merry. "I said how he had feelings for her. That ain't the same thing as . . . as . . . You need to get your mind out of the gutter, Missy! Now, move it. Mr Holdsworth doesn't like being kept waiting."

I found Mr Holdsworth in the butler's pantry. He was standing over a small table that had obviously been brought in specially as it made the room quite overcrowded. It was strewn with small cards. The Butler was wearing a very worried expression and mopping his brow frequently with his handkerchief. His expression lightened as I came into the room. "Euphemia! Wonderful! Now, this is a long shot, but do you by any chance have any knowledge of dining etiquette? Particularly who should be seated by whom?"

"A little," I said nervously.

"Good! Good! Come in then. I thought my knowledge of such matters was adequate, but this is such a large event. Which members of the nobility does an archdeacon take precedence over precisely?"

"Shouldn't Lady Stapleford be doing this?"

"Mrs Wilson normally does the seating plan."

"Ah," I said, looking the Butler square in the eye.

Holdsworth dropped his gaze. "You haven't been here long, Euphemia. Things aren't as black and white as you imagine."

"You're shielding her."

"Yes. Now, can you help or not?"

I admit I was strongly tempted to turn round, trot up the stairs and deliver Mrs Wilson up to her Mistress on one of the silver platters she had me polish late into the night.

There are disadvantages, many disadvantages, to being raised in a vicarage. The indoctrination of the notion of Christian charity, while obviously a moral advantage, carries with it the heavy disadvantages of duty and commitment to selflessness.

I sat down next to the Butler. "You've almost got that right, but these two need swapping."

Mr Holdsworth sighed a sigh that came up from the depths of his boots. "But that leaves the Wirthington brothers next to each other and they haven't spoken in years."

"Rank must override personal considerations," I spoke with my mother's authority. "But we will see what we can do. Tell me about these people and we will attempt to contrive a peaceful seating arrangement."

And tell me he did. Even though Mr Holdsworth knew little of seating plans, he knew the ins and outs of all the guests down to some extremely intimate details. Although to give him credit, he alluded rather than putting me to the blush. It took us half an hour.

"I am deeply impressed, Euphemia. This is a most happy outcome."

"I'm not sure it is precisely happy," I answered, "but it both satisfies the proprieties and seems least likely to lead to conflict."

"Where did you learn all this?"

"From my mother."

"Your mother? Who are you?"

I sat back in my chair. My eyes were burning from staring at the tiny copperplate script on the place cards. "I don't suppose it matters now. I doubt I will be employed here tomorrow."

"You have done me a great favour, Euphemia. If tonight does not go well, then all our jobs are in jeopardy. All the staff will be grateful to you."

I snorted in a manner that would have made my mother faint. "I think the staff generally have a very low opinion of me."

"I never thought the worse of you."

This was so kindly said I could feel tears pricking at the back of my eyes. "I'm the granddaughter of an Earl," I blurted out. "He disinherited my mother when she married beneath her. My father was a vicar."

"So you are a mixture of propriety and nobility," said Mr Holdsworth. "And a credit, if I may make so bold, to both your parents. I take it that financial circumstances drove you into service when your father died?"

"I have a little brother."

"If you will forgive me saying so, the cruelty of your grandfather has obviously not descended down the generations."

I felt a tell tale blush wash over me. Since Father died, no one had spoken to me at length and so kindly. It was very tempting to lean my head on Mr Holdsworth's shoulder and shed a few maidenly tears. But having admitted to being an Earl's granddaughter, I could hardly weep over a Butler.

"Families can be very cruel," said Mr Holdsworth. "My niece . . ."

What he was to say next was lost as a commotion broke out above us. Angry male voices sparred loudly. I could not make out the words, but I heard Mr Bertram's voice.

"Mr Holdsworth, I have to go. I must see Mr Bertram."

The Butler's eyes widened in alarm. He held out a hand to me, "Euphemia," he began, but he reached into empty air. I was already running from the room.

"The business! Damn the business! Shipping guns to Africa to slaughter natives! You call that trade?"

"Morality, little half-brother! It doesn't suit you. You can't fool me. If you were this bothered you would have left the house long ago."

"I stayed for Father!"

"Balderdash. You couldn't stand the man! None of us could. Not even the Mater."

I flew up the stairs, but slowed when I was almost at the top. Could I really break in on the brothers' argument? I fully intended to leave once the murder had been solved. I no longer considered myself a servant. If I am honest, I thought of myself as an agent of Mr Bertram, but I was under no illusions that he would agree with me. And I had no doubt whatsoever that to Mr Richard I was no more than an irritating and insignificant maid. What worried me was exactly how irritating I might be to him and what he might do about it. The last thing I wanted to do was attract his attention, but I knew what I had was important. I moved slowly up the stairs. If I stood at the edge of the hall I would hopefully attract the right brother's attention.

The quarrel reached a white hot level, or in Mr Richard's case a sort of suffused purple. "Damn you, man. You dare preach morality to me when you're keeping that little whore in my house and expecting me to pay for her." He flung an accusatory finger in my direction. So much for staying out of sight. I stepped into Mr Bertram's direct eye-line.

"Excuse me," I began, "I really need to talk to . . ."

"Get back to the kitchen, wench," bellowed Mr Richard.

"Euphemia," cried Mr Bertram in an exasperated manner. "Now is not the time."

"But . . ."

Both men turned their full attention on me and in a sudden show of accord shouted, "Go!"

I confess I was not proofed against such ill

nature. I picked up my skirts and fled down the stairs. Above me the argument raged out, and to my shame, my name was frequently mentioned. At the bottom of the stairs I almost ran into Mr Holdsworth.

"Perhaps now would be a good time for you to post that letter. It might be wise to let things settle a little."

I did not need persuading. Stopping for no longer than to collect my coat and the missive, within minutes I was walking down the drive. The air was sharp and fresh. Around me the quietude of nature cast its spell on my soul. My pulse slowed and my breathing became more even. My colour returned to normal. I could feel a weight lifted from my shoulders. I had the ridiculous feeling that should I jump into the air I would not come down for some time. Outside of Stapleford Hall, I was as light as a feather.

I walked across the fields with a measured pace. I knew I would be missed and chastised if I was too long, but I lingered as much as I dared. It was all too soon that I came upon the village.

As I approached, an older lady in a very yellow hat, carrying a wicker basket, went into the post office. I followed quietly in behind her. As soon as I stepped inside, this lady and the woman serving behind the counter, a lady in middle age and an unsuitable summer floral flock, turned their attention full on me.

"How can I help?" said the woman behind the counter.

"I've a letter to post, if I could buy a stamp?'

The woman with the basket was watching me closely. "Are you from up the Hall?"

I nodded. "I'm the new maid at the Hall."

The two women exchanged looks. "Is something wrong?" I asked politely.

"Not at all, love," said the postmistress. She handed me the stamp. "Do you want me to put this in the collection for you?"

"Thank you," I said, watching uneasily as she read the address.

"Looking for a new situation?" asked the basket woman.

I shook my head. I knew enough of village ways to realise I was being asked to provide a story, and a good one. "No, I'm writing to my old employer. She asked me to let her know when I was settled. She moved into a smaller establishment and let me go. Her son took over the big house and I didn't fancy working for him."

"Out of the frying pan and into the fire!" exclaimed the basket woman. The woman behind the counter hushed her.

"Ladies," I said calmly and with as much respect as I could muster, "if there is something

I should know about Stapleford Hall, I would be grateful if you would tell me. I am new to the area and my own mother has passed away. I do not have anyone to advise me."

The two women exchanged looks again. This was becoming tiresome. "Please," I begged prettily.

"I don't hold with gossip," said the postmistress. "I have the standard of the post office to uphold."

The woman with the basket looked faintly disappointed. "Of course," I said politely. I wished them both a good day and left. Outside I made a pretence of retying my shoe and within moments, as I had hoped, the basket woman rushed out. She touched me lightly on the arm and drew me to one side.

She nodded towards the post office. "She's afraid of upsetting the gentry. But they're not real gentry. They're new and what with all that's happening, I think a pretty young thing like you should be warned."

I nodded eagerly.

"Well, I know how I shouldn't be saying anything what with that murder and all, but do you know what happened to the last maid?"

I shook my head. Basket woman leaned in and spoke very softly, "Got into trouble she did." She stood back and nodded at me several times.

"Oh," I said as the realisation dawned. "That kind of trouble."

"Just a wee bit of girl she was and it killed her. The babe survived, but none of them would have anything to do with it. Girl's mother is beside herself. They're local like and it's created a lot of ill will."

"Whose?"

"She never said. Might have been the shame. Might have been she hoped how he'd claim her or at least give her some money for the babe if she held her tongue. Much good it did her."

"That's very sad."

The basket woman heaved up her basket more securely into her arms. "She should have kept her skirt down. But there, she's paid a heavy price."

I fought down my anger. I knew my opinion would not be popular. "What was her name?"

"Lucy," said the woman. "Lucy something. She was a relation of one of the others on the staff on her father's side. He's long gone. Can't remember who it was, but they got her the position. Pity they didn't look out for her more. But there I've done my Christian duty, you're forewarned. If anything happens no one can say I didn't do my part."

With that she raised her nose in the air, gave a triumphal snort and headed off.

"Lucy," I whispered to myself. "Lucy died and the babe survived."

An Uncomfortable Position

My head was in a whirl. Those place cards. That spidery writing. I'd seen it before. Holdsworth saying "my niece". The look on his face. I was fitting pieces of the puzzle together, but instead of the satisfaction I had hoped for, a growing dread was filling my heart.

I was half way back to the Hall before I realised it. A loud bark jolted me from my revelry. The thicket ahead rustled loudly and then emerged a familiar wolfhound.

"Siegfried, where are you?" called Richenda's voice from behind the hedge.

"He's here, Miss Richenda," I answered.

Miss Richenda popped up on a stile. She froze for a moment. "Don't be scared, Euphemia. He won't hurt you," her tone was not confident.

She hopped down the step and hurried towards me. By the time she arrived, Siegfried and I were happily renewing our acquaintance. "Well, he certainly seems to like you." There was a note of jealously in her voice.

I smiled. "I like dogs. We used to keep them," I blushed under her curious gaze. "I was brought up in the country."

"You're quite full of surprises." Her lips curled in a cold smile. "Can't stand them myself. This beast belongs to Bertram." Then her expression warmed. "Men! They are such a great nuisance, aren't they? Swanning off to London and leaving me to look after his dog."

"It does sometimes seem life would be simpler if things were run by women," I said.

Miss Richenda positively beamed. "A girl after my own heart."

"It is hard for women, sometimes, isn't it?"

"What do you mean?"

"Oh, I don't know. Just some men can be difficult. You must see a lot of that in your work. With the shelters."

"Men don't only make bastards," Miss Richenda said darkly.

"You feel sorry for those women?"

"Of course. Us lot, even you, have it easy compared to the streetwalkers in London." I had never felt more in sympathy with her. I took a deep breath.

"Does it ever get, well, close to home?"

She flicked me a glance. "You've been listening to backstairs gossip." She paused as if considering and then leaning closer said, "Between you and me, the man was a dreadful cad. Terrible influence on my brother."

I shook my head. We walked in silence for a short while. "I replaced Mr Holdsworth's niece, didn't I?"

Miss Richenda frowned. "Possibly. I wasn't really on speaking terms with my honourable parents until recently."

"Oh."

"Just like the fairy stories. Never got on with my sainted stepmother."

"That must have been hard."

Miss Richenda shrugged. "We all have our crosses."

The Hall came into sight over the ridge. I took a deep breath. "Do you know if Holdsworth's niece was called Lucy?"

Miss Richenda stopped. "Spit it out!"

"I'm sorry?"

"Just stop beating around the bush and say whatever it is that's on your mind."

"It's all so difficult," I said pathetically.

Miss Richenda clapped me firmly on the shoulder. "Don't know who to trust, do you? Poor little thing. Tell me. Girls together and all that."

"I'm afraid Holdsworth killed Mr George. His niece died in childbirth bearing a bastard."

"And you think it was Georgie's?"

"I wondered. If Holdsworth was mad with grief . . . But I can't imagine him killing your father."

"Gosh, you have got yourself in a pickle. I think you should talk to Bertram. Richard was, well, caught up with Georgie. Come on up to my room. You can wait there. If we put our heads together we might be able to sort some of this out."

I felt a little shiver down my back, like an army of ants in icicle boots. I nodded.

Miss Richenda whipped me in by the side door. She left the dog downstairs and we made our way quietly to her room. "Make yourself comfortable," she smiled and closed the door.

Then I heard the sound of the key in the lock and knew I had made a dreadful mistake. As my father would have said, there's ethics and then there's family. All too often one will override the other.

I ran to the window. It was unlocked. I threw up the pane and poked my head out. The gravelled drive below seemed a very long way down. Unfortunately the house was too new to have any established ivy and a quick check revealed no nearby drainpipes.

I struggled with my emotions. It would have felt heroic and daring to climb out of the window, but I had not done anything of this nature since I was twelve, and long skirts were most hampering. On the one hand I felt I should rescue myself, but on the other hand I felt it was really time Mr Bertram pulled his socks up and got down to being manly in the defence of justice – i.e. rescuing me.

It was not long before I heard the sound of the key in the lock once more. I retreated behind the bed. Miss Richenda entered followed by her twin. "I'm sorry, Euphemia. You know I don't have a high opinion of the male animal in general, but this one is my twin and to be frank, he has to take prescience over my half-brother's troublesome new mistress."

"*New* mistress?" I echoed blankly.

"Oh dear. Young lady," said Mr Richard, advancing towards me, "you didn't think my young brother was priestly in nature, did you?"

I clutched the edge of the bedspread. It was silky and cool. One of my nails caught in the lace edging. "If you lay a hand on me I will scream!"

Mr Richard swept a pile of books, notebooks and stockings off the bedroom chair and sat down. Miss Richenda hovered by the doorway.

"Now why on earth should I do that?" asked

Mr Richard. "I assure you, my brother and I do not share similar tastes."

"Let me go. I won't tell anyone."

"Tell them what?" asked my tormentor.

"Anything!"

"Then you will have to be singularly silent. I wonder how we might arrange that?" He smiled at me in much the manner of a fox spying a hen house. "Now what was it this little tattle tale said that bothered you, Sis?"

"She thinks Georgie knocked up Holdsworth's niece and he killed him for it."

I blushed scarlet.

"Hush, Sis. You're upsetting our guest. She isn't one of your whores. This is a more classy piece." He directed his gaze back at me. "So you're spreading gossip about my father's staff, are you wench? And why did Holdsworth kill the Pater then?"

I swallowed. "I don't think he did." My voice sounded very small.

Mr Richard nodded. "Clever girl. Someone taking advantage of the situation. That's what you think, isn't it?" The expression on my face must have been most legible, for he continued, "Surprised are you, my dear? Not a card player then. Yes, I do have something of a brain."

"Richard, why do you think Holdsworth killed Papa?"

He turned his calm blue eyes towards her. "Oh, I think, my dear, he felt that Pater should have protected the staff in his care better." He paused. "Or maybe Pater had been too interested in his staff."

"Richard, no!"

"Don't be squeamish, Richenda. You know what Father was like with women."

"But not at home!"

Mr Richard shrugged. "It doesn't matter, does it? He's dead. We're the ones who count now. We need this neat and tidy."

"But you don't have any proof!" I blurted out.

"Richenda, gag her and stuff her in the wardrobe."

I should have run at that very moment, but the way he spoke, as calmly as he might order a post-prandial brandy, caught me off guard. My brain told me I had misheard even as Miss Richenda stuffed a hankie in my mouth whilst her brother bound my hands with the curtain tie. I am happy to say I ripped the bedspread as they dragged me across the room. Then they both bundled me into the wardrobe.

I slumped to the floor, shaking in the darkness as I heard someone lock the wardrobe door.

"Is this wise?" asked Miss Richenda.

"I'm thinking this might be just the bargaining

chip we need to bring Bertram onside."

"Oh Brother, you are clever."

Hot tears spilled down my cheeks.

Now this was the point at which I should have succumbed to maidenly hysterics, but I had already had a most exhausting day. The shock at discovering Mr Holdsworth might be a murderer, the long winter walk, my idiocy at confiding in Miss Richenda and her subsquent betrayal and the rough handling that had placed me in this dress-filled prison had taken their toll. So, despite the unpleasant fact that Miss Richenda's last maid had obviously not been skilled in laundry services and Miss Richenda being a plump, but active young woman, I did something I had never done before. I trusted in someone else. As I closed my eyes in exhaustion, I trusted in Mr Bertram to rescue me.

I awoke sometime later, unrescued, with a painful cramp in my left leg. Outside I could hear the sound of automobiles and carriages. The guests were gathering for the evening event. It was late and clearly no white knight was on the horizon. I began to work at the rope around my wrist. It was very tight.

Then the bedroom door opened. I held my breath.

"Come on, Merry. I've hardly any time to get ready!"

I rained silent curses on Mr Bertram's head.

"Certainly, Miss Richenda. I'll do my best. I can't think what's happened to Euphemia."

"Probably gone. A bit of a fly-by-night if you ask me."

"Yes, Miss."

"Indeed, I believe the police are still considering her a suspect."

"Oh no, Miss! That I can't believe."

In the darkness I was desperately counting the odds. If I kicked on the door, would Merry come to my aid? Miss Richenda was larger, but Merry worked harder every day of her life than Miss Richenda would ever do in a month. If I made a lot of noise, Merry would respond. What could Miss Richenda say? She'd already said she didn't know where I was. Would I be endangering Merry or was this my only chance? If Miss Richenda was suggesting I had left, I could not suppress the chilling thought she was laying the ground for my disappearance. I hunched myself as far into the corner as possible, flexed my cramped limbs and readied myself to kick as hard as I could against the oak door. Two dresses fell down on my head.

"What was that?" asked Merry. "Sounded like something in your wardrobe."

"Nothing," said Miss Richenda in a loud, clear voice. "I've overfilled it as usual. Now, Merry, I think I should do this bit. Those hairpins are very

sharp. I wouldn't want you to hurt yourself."
The last two words were said with unnecessary
emphasis. I hesitated.

"No, Miss, but they're just hairpins."

"One of the girls who came to the shelter
claimed she had killed her . . . er . . . owner with
one."

"No, Miss! Really! Is that possible?"

"I imagine there is only one way one could
find out."

I froze. I couldn't quite believe she would do
it, but then if someone had told me I would be
embroiled in murder within minutes of entering
service I would never have believed that either.

"Well I never, Miss. In that case, I'll let you
finish. Would you like me to tidy up your room
while you're at the party? It does need a bit of
straightening."

"Rubbish," snapped Miss Richenda, "it's
homely. Just how I like it. Besides, Mrs Wilson
would skin me alive if I didn't get you back
downstairs quick sharp. That must be the fifth
automobile I've heard pull up in as many
minutes."

"As you wish, Miss."

With a sinking heart I listened to them both
leave.

I had no options left. I kicked hard at the
wardrobe door. I succeeded only in making a

loud noise and bruising my foot. But then what is a little pain when you think your life is in mortal peril? I struck again and again, but sadly the wardrobe was of excellent craftsmanship.

When it was clear nothing more than my own exhaustion could be accomplished, I stopped. Everyone was downstairs now. No one would hear. I needed a plan for when they came to get me. I guessed it would be late this evening, possibly even into the early hours of the morrow, when all the celebrants would be the worse for wear.

The twins were large and powerful. Surprise would be my only advantage. They would be expecting a timid, frightened girl. I might be feeling exactly that inside, but I determined they would never suspect my fear. I had my pride. Unfortunately, that appeared to be all I had. I began to scrabble around on the floor of the wardrobe, feeling the dresses as best I could with my bound hands. Even a stray pin plunged into a fleshy part of one of my captors might give me those few moments of shock that could mean the difference between life and death.

Then the bedroom door opened. The thought that they might attempt to dispose of me whilst the party was in full swing crept terrifyingly into my mind. At that moment, my hands closed on the smooth coldness of a pin. Quickly, I pried it free with my nails. It wasn't much, but it was a chance.

The wardrobe swung open. I blinked, momentarily dazzled by the gaslight. "Merry!" I grunted in astonishment through my gag. "Merry!"

"Just what are you doing in there?" chided my rescuer. "You're going to get her dresses all . . . is that a gag?"

Her swift fingers had it off me in a trice. Then she was helping me out and tutting over my bonds. She fetched a pair of scissors from Miss Richenda's dressing table and with difficulty began to cut through the curtain cord. "I'm not sure I want to know what's happening here."

"How did you know I was in there?" I gasped. I pulled my hands apart and rubbed my sore wrists.

"You smell of onions."

"Mrs Wilson made me chop . . ."

"Yes, I know," interrupted Merry, "but Miss Richenda's room doesn't or shouldn't."

"You are clever, Merry," I said with heartfelt sincerity.

"I'm clever enough to know I don't want to know what you're up to."

"It's nothing terrible! I . . . "

Merry held up her hand. "Sssh! Whatever's going on, I don't want to know. Is there anyone who can get you out of this pickle? The Police Inspector?"

I shook my head. "Mr Bertram."

Merry placed her hands on my shoulders. "Look, we haven't always seen eye to eye, but after what happened to Lucy . . . I'll always blame myself for that."

"What happened?"

"She never said who it was. It's all water under the bridge now. But I don't want to see another maid harmed by this family. My own family's not far from here. They've not got much, but I'm sure Ma would take you in for a bit while you got on your feet if I asked her."

Tears stung my eyes. "That's really kind of you. But no, I need to speak to Mr Bertram – only speak. I'm not what the rest of you think. I've never been . . . but I know too much of what's going on here. He's the only one of the family I can trust."

Merry watched me appraisingly. "I reckon you've got that right. He's the only apple in the barrel that's not rotten through." She thought for a moment. "Tell you what, my sister's husband runs the inn down at the village. If you say you've come from me he'll let you stay there. You've got some coin, right?"

I nodded. "Good, 'cos he's a stingy sod. You'll have to get your stuff too. I can't ask him to take someone that don't seem . . ." She let the sentence trail off.

"You're right," I said, though I knew it would cost me precious time. "Will you let him know where I am?"

"Of course. Though I'm not sure I should."

I placed a hand over one of hers. "Merry, this is serious," I said. "It's a matter of life and death."

We stood there for a moment. Between us I felt a silent understanding, a comradeship of servants. My heart turned over. Now, when I had to go, I had finally found how to fit in. Then Merry shrugged, stepped back and dropped her hands from my shoulders. "It'll be my life if Mrs Wilson catches me skiving off. She's never as narky as when she's coming out of one of her little tea drinking phases." I walked quickly to the door.

" 'Ang on! Let me check the coast is clear."

She pushed past me and pulled open the door, stuck out her head and then frantically waved me through. I ran down the corridor towards the servants' stairs. Once on them, I felt a modicum of safety.

I fairly flew up to my room. The upper reaches of the house were silent. Far below I could hear the sounds of merriment. I stuck my sole rickety chair under the door handle and began to pack like a woman possessed.

I was in the process of closing my bags when the chair suddenly shot across the room as the door swung violently open.

What the Butler Knew

"I warn you. I am armed!"

I raised the candlestick above my head. I did my best to think valiant thoughts, but my legs trembled under my long skirts. Hot wax dripped onto my sleeve and there was a smell of burning.

"Euphemia! Are you safe? Merry has just told me the most outlandish story about you being shut in a cupboard," Mr Bertram burst into the room. His eyes travelled to the flame above my head. "Put that down before you set the whole place on fire."

"Oh thank the Lord," I began. Mr Bertram removed the implement from my slackened grasp before I managed to do more than mildly singe my hair.

"Why didn't you blow it out?" he

demanded.

"How could I have seen my assailant otherwise?"

"That is ridiculous."

I bridled under his scorn. "Where were you when they locked me in the wardrobe?"

"London."

"No you weren't. You were arguing with your brother in the hallway. You both shouted at me!"

"Then I was just back from London!"

"You should have been looking for me!"

Mr Bertram gritted his teeth. "I do not believe there was any possibility that I could have foreseen you would get yourself locked in a cupboard."

"A wardrobe! A wardrobe with pungent dresses!"

He picked up the fallen chair, righted it, dumped it down harshly and threw himself down upon it with a petulant flap of his coat-tails. "A wardrobe then! Good God girl. I have a lot on my mind. My father and cousin have been murdered."

I stamped my foot. "Better things to think about than me, you mean!"

I had gone too far. The anger faded from his face and Mr Bertram gave me a look of complete incomprehension. "What are you talking about, Euphemia?"

I found myself gulping air in a most unladylike

manner as I tried to compose myself. "I thought we were in this together."

"Together?" The blankness of his tone pierced through me.

"A team," I said quietly. "For justice."

Mr Bertram threw back his head and laughed. "You are the most unusual maid, my dear. But really, it wouldn't be seemly for us to be, as you put it, a team."

"Because women don't get involved in these matters?" I ventured.

"That and because of the disparity of our stations."

I was about to respond that this didn't bother me one bit, when reality washed over me like cold water. I had been behaving like my father's daughter, maybe even like my mother's, but to him I was not the respectable daughter of a rural vicar or the estranged granddaughter of an Earl, I was a maid with upstairs responsibilities. That I had no one to blame for this but myself was the hardest part to bear.

I swallowed hard and curtsied. "I'm sorry, Sir. I forgot myself."

Mr Bertram coughed. "I don't mean to say you haven't been helpful, Euphemia. I do appreciate your help. I know little of the world below stairs and your insight has been most valuable."

I curtsied again. This was it. No apology for

what his brother had done or the danger in which I had been placed. Mr Bertram reached inside his trouser pocket. I quailed. For one awful moment I thought he was going to produce a shilling.

"The thing is, Euphemia, it turns out it was nothing to do with the servants at all. I'll tell you this, but mum's the word until I officially let the cat out of the bag."

I sat down on the bed and folded my hands neatly in my lap. I could not help glancing at the door occasionally, but Mr Bertram seemed to have no fear of interruption. Hopefully, this time he would intervene if someone tried to put me in a wardrobe again. It had finally sunk into my befuddled brain that I would need this man's help to get away from his brother and sister.

Mr Bertram leaned forward on his seat. "You see, the thing is, it turns out both Richard and George were syphoning money off the old man's bank."

"Bank?"

Mr Bertram waved his hand. "Yes. Father had a small bank as well as the armament business. I've spoken to the family lawyer. He took a bit of persuading, but he eventually told me, because I'm my father's executor and will have to sort out the mess, that George and Richard had been syphoning off the funds. He never let Richard work in the armament business. Seems Pater never entirely trusted him. It explains why he was always so ragingly furious that I wouldn't go into it. Richard had high hopes though that my father would let him in. Especially if he pulled off a deal of his own. He and George were using his mother's name to trade on. It's all a bit unpleasant. I won't bore you with the entire details, suffice it to say this company wanted more than Richard could borrow from the bank without anyone noticing. So he took what he could and speculated. Lost the lot."

"So he killed George and your father to cover his tracks?"

"I don't think that was it. From what I could get that clam-faced lawyer to say, my father already knew. He was dealing with it, but holding the whole incident over Richard as a guarantee of good behaviour – essentially doing whatever Pater wanted."

"I can see he would not like that. But why would he kill George?"

"No," Bertram paused, "Richard is ambitious. He wanted to be in Parliament. There were two people between him and the parliamentary seat and now there aren't."

I had little doubt that Richard had killed his father. It all fitted very neatly, but I was equally sure he had not murdered George. My inner demon prompted me to be quiet, but my conscience urged me to speak.

"I don't think you have it quite right."

"Oh really?"

"I think your brother did murder your father. He almost admitted as much to me, but I don't think he killed George. I think he took advantage of the situation. I think the Butler did it."

"Holdsworth?"

"Your brother is going to blame him for both murders."

"Holdsworth? Why? He's been with us for years."

"Did you know that your last maid, Lucy, left because she was with child?"

Mr Bertram blushed. "No, I did not. I had no idea. I cannot discuss this with you!"

"Suitable topic of conversation or not, it's true. Lucy died in childbirth. The babe survived. The grandmother has it. Apparently, gossip in the village says she petitioned someone at the Hall for aid, but was refused."

"Of course I'll see to it she gets help, Euphemia, but . . ."

"She was Holdsworth's niece."

"Ah," said Mr Bertram.

"But you may be right," I added quickly. "Richard might have killed both men."

Mr Bertram gave me an appraising look. "Much as your conscience prompted you to tell me this, I suspect it would also suggest that murder cannot be condoned even by a righteous man."

I hung my head. "No," I agreed softly. "But Richard is going to blame both murders on Holdsworth!"

"That doesn't surprise me in the least. My brother is as amoral as he is stupid. He never thinks things through properly."

"I think he is cleverer than most people give him credit for. He certainly has cunning."

Mr Bertram rose with the air of a man bent on decisive action. "I feel sorry for Holdsworth, but I will not conceal what you have told me. I have enough evidence from the lawyer and with his imprisonment of you to open the Inspector's eyes to Richard's true nature. I will send for the Inspector now. He can join us at dinner and Richard will be revealed for what he is."

"No, don't," I blurted out. "That's such a dramatic plan, it's bound to go wrong."

Mr Bertram raised an eyebrow. "I think you can leave me to handle such matters, Euphemia. I must ask you to remain in the attic. I may need to call upon your testimony. I will ensure Richard and his twin are in my sight at all times. You will not be in danger."

"Mr Bertram, please, I don't think this is the wisest course of action."

"You will have to let me be the judge of that," he said and closed the door quietly behind him.

A thousand thoughts rushed through my mind and none of them were welcome. Mr Bertram's plan suited his sense of the dramatic, but Mr Richard was a wilier character than he gave him credit for. I feared Holdsworth would end up charged with both murders. I could not let that happen. I grabbed a paper and pen, scribbled a short note and despite Mr Bertram's command, I left the room.

The upper house was still in silence. I made my way down the servants' stairs. At the bottom, I peeked cautiously around the corner. I could hear Mrs Deighton's voice coming from the kitchen: something about the softness of modern cauliflowers. Merry's voice murmured in response. I knew Mr Holdsworth would be busy upstairs serving cocktails. I darted across the hallway and into the butler's pantry. It was empty as I had hoped. Now, where could I leave Holdsworth a note that only he would find? No one else would normally come in here, but if he was under suspicion might not the police search here? And I had accused Mr Bertram of not thinking things through. I had to get the note to him before the police became suspicious, but how?

I have been brought up to believe that God

answers one's prayers, but not always in the way one expects - more often than not He says "no". My father always held God had a sense of humour, so I hope he was watching my expression when the pantry door opened and Mr Holdsworth entered.

Our eyes met. "You know, don't you?" said the Butler.

"Yes."

Mr Holdsworth came into the room. He shut the door behind him and leant upon it. I could not help but be aware that the only other potential exit was a small window that was heavily barred.

"Why are you here?"

"I came to warn you." I held out the note. "But I couldn't think of where to hide it."

Mr Holdsworth took it and read, "Mr Richard knows about Lucy. He intends to accuse you of both murders, though I fear he murdered his father himself. You must go at once." He looked up, blinking back tears. "You know about my Lucy?"

"I pieced it together. Gossip here and there."

The Butler slammed his fists down upon the table. "Damn it! Damn it!" I flinched. Then he turned to me. "You mustn't think badly of her. It's worse than you know. He forced himself on her."

"I didn't . . ." I began but he wasn't listening

to me.

"I found her afterwards. She blamed herself. Said she should never have let herself be alone with him. He'd told her men have urges."

"The beast," I whispered beneath my breath. Holdsworth nodded violently. "And then when she finds she is pregnant and he tells her if she keeps on . . . if she keeps on . . . he'll see she is all right."

"My God! What a monster."

"I went to the Mistress, but she wouldn't hear a word of it. And Lucy, Lucy said it was better that way. The babe would have a future. But he tired of her. Sent her back to her mother without a penny. Then she dies and he does nothing."

"So you thought you'd blackmail him? I found part of your note in the grate. Why did you use that? You must have realised someone would notice. It's never used."

"Time. I didn't have time," he muttered. His eyes had a faraway look and he hardly seemed to be aware of my presence. "I kept thinking about Lucy as a tiny mite, sitting on my knee in her favourite blue dress and begging for a kitten. She never got one. And my sister, I couldn't bear it."

To my alarm he choked back a sob. The poor man was overwrought – as overwrought as I imagine he was when he confronted George.

"I'm so deeply sorry, Holdsworth," I said

sincerely.

"Thank you. I know you are. You're not like them." He wiped his eyes on the back of his hands. "How did you know it was me?"

His question echoed loudly in my mind. It is one thing to have suspicions and quite another to have them confirmed. "I guessed you arranged to meet and things didn't work out as planned."

He laughed once, a short, mirthless bark, that chilled me to the core. "Didn't work out as planned? How do you know I didn't mean to kill him all along?"

The floor swam beneath me. I gripped the edge of the table. "I don't believe you're an evil man, Mr Holdsworth. I believe you are a wronged and bereaved one. A man, who might be moved to anger by indifference."

"You're very acute, Euphemia. It says a lot about our world that you are in service – a girl as bright and good as you shouldn't be forced to serve her betters." He spat the last word violently into the air between us. "Do you know what he did when I met him?"

I shook my head.

"He laughed in my face. I'd only taken the knife to frighten him. He said Lucy was a little whore who'd got no more than she deserved, so I pushed him into the passage and stabbed him. It didn't take him long to die. Not long enough at all."

"Did you search my room?" Mr Holdsworth shook his head. "It must have been Mr Richard," I said, thinking aloud. "He must have suspected George was being blackmailed over something and thought I'd taken a blackmail letter off the body, so I could blackmail the family too! Really! How could he imagine I would be so dishonest!"

"I'm sorry you got caught up in this, Euphemia."

I felt my limbs go leaden. "What do you mean?" I whispered. "What are you going to do?"

"Do?" asked Holdsworth. "I'm going to give myself up. What else can I do?"

"No," I cried. "He'll lay both murders at your door and get away scot-free. You'll be sacrificed as Lucy was! You can't, you can't give up."

Mr Holdsworth stepped away from the door and sat down. "There isn't anything else you can do."

I reached into the pocket of my skirt and pulled out my coins. "Here, take these. Go. Go abroad. No one's looking for you. You can make it to the coast. Start a new life."

"How can I leave my sister and the babe?"

"You'll be no use to them hanging from a noose. Hasn't your sister suffered enough? Besides, I made Mr Bertram promise he'd see them right. He's a good man. His word counts. Come on, Holdsworth, you can't want your sister to suffer this too. You can't let those bastards win!"

The Right Honourable Member

I flew up the stairs, but I was too late. I had taken too long. I had not reached the top before I heard the voice of Mr Bertram greeting the Inspector in the hallway. I stopped short.

"Come up to the library, Inspector. I have information I need to share with you."

I could hear the hearty chink of glasses and the occasional loud laugh in the distance. The party was in full swing. They must be about to sit down to dine at any moment. The Inspector appeared to think so too.

"I'd rather not, Sir. Don't want to intrude on Sir Richard's big night. Last I heard a landslide success was expected. So unless you've got the murderer upstairs in your library, I'll see you in the morning."

Mr Bertram laughed. "Oh no, Inspector, he's not in the library, but he will be dining here later."

"If this is some kind of a joke?"

"Indeed not."

"Then I'll need to use your phone and call for more men."

"He's right here, Inspector."

"You sure about this, Sir? It wouldn't be good for either of us if you were wrong."

"The murderer is in this house right now. I have incontrovertible evidence."

I thought this was laying it on a bit thick. Mr Bertram might have proof of embezzlement, but little more. However, it seemed the Inspector was getting carried away by Mr Bertram's enthusiasm.

I bolted back down the stairs. No wonder servants lived to a ripe old age. We certainly got more exercise than our more sedate employers. We didn't get to go to posh dinners. The sound of the party had reminded me I hadn't eaten since breakfast and I was famished.

I needed to get to the passage behind the library. The easiest way was to go through the kitchen, but I did not believe it likely I could get by there unchallenged. Instead, I took a different route. I was fairly sure the passageway from the drawing room wound up towards the library.

Unfortunately, my normally excellent sense of direction became somewhat challenged in the dim light of the servants' ways and it took me far longer than it should have done until I finally arrived at the library entrance.

I pressed my ear to the crack and listened.

"Don't you see, Inspector, the money he took from the bank had to be repaid?"

"And he used this money to buy shares in this Frenchie company?"

"No," I could hear the exasperation in Mr Bertram's voice. "He was buying favours – bribes. He needed both more money and influence to gain a serious stake in the French company. He dabbled in speculation and lost even more."

"A seat in Parliament would be helpful then?"

"Exactly."

"And do you have any proof of this embezzlement?"

"Yes."

"I'm still not clear in my head as to why he killed your cousin."

Mr Bertram hesitated. Then he spoke, "They were in it together. The whole scheme."

"No honour among thieves then." The Inspector cleared his throat. "This must be a very difficult time for you, Sir."

"Not been the best days of my life."

The Inspector made an odd coughing noise again. "Er, I was just thinking how it might be easy to make mistakes when one is overwrought. Grief can do that. My wife, when she lost her mother . . ."

"Here. These are papers from the bank. I have charge of it under the terms of my father's will until probate is done. The family lawyer is downstairs. He's been collecting more proofs for me."

"Right. Right. Embezzlement's not my area. But I'll have a word with the man. If you don't mind me saying, Sir, and with all due respect, there's a big step between a bit of dodgy dealing and killing your own father . . ."

Suddenly I became aware of an excruciating pain in my left ear. Then I was yanked backwards. Two black eyes glittered at me in the dimness and a sour smell washed over me. "What do you think you're doing, girl?" snapped Mrs Wilson.

"Could you let go of my ear, please. That hurts very much."

"Don't you go thinking I'm going to let you get away again. You've been skiving this whole day. Believe me, if I could find anyone else I would. This way."

"If you could let go of my ear I could walk more quickly."

But Mrs Wilson paid me no attention. She

hauled me along towards the kitchen in a manner that convinced me that at any moment I would lose the appendage. I considered kicking her, but even as I readied my balance for the action she dug her nails hard into my ear lobe. I felt a trickle of fresh blood. I am certain at that moment in such circumstances Merry would have sworn at her, but I held to the last threads of my dignity. I hoped one day to wear earrings.

When we reached the kitchen she released me and shoved me forward.

"She'll have to do," said Mrs Wilson.

A red-faced Mrs Deighton looked up from between the pots. "Lord-a-lummie, you can't let a maid go serving in there."

"As we seem to have a sudden scarcity of serving gentlemen, I have little option. At least this one has more grace than Merry. She's used enough to mixing above her station to manage to serve a few potatoes, as long as she keeps her legs together."

I flushed scarlet and rounded on Mrs Wilson. "How dare you? You harridan!"

"Harridan am I? Well, there's far worse words for the likes of you!"

A bell rang urgently. Then another.

"Oh lor," said Mrs Deighton. "Merry, you'll have to do."

"I can't," stammered Merry. "Don't ask me,

please, don't ask me. Euphemia!" She turned her big eyes towards me in wretched appeal.

How could I refuse her? If she had not released me from my sartorial prison, I might not now have the breath to harangue Wilson.

"For you, Merry," I said grandly, and lifted the large serving dish from the table.

Merry need not have worried. Upstairs was a glitter of candlelight and crystal. All the leaves of the great table had been inserted. The room was packed with people and incredibly hot. What passed for elegant conversation flowed in harmony with the deluge of wine. The air was heavy with the scent of perfume and sour sweat. No one was paying the least attention to the servants. They were all intent on impressing their neighbours.

Mr Bertram slipped into the back of the room and tapped an uncomfortable-looking man in worn evening dress on the shoulder. He got up at once and followed him out. I surmised that was the lawyer.

I made my way around serving the ladies. "Potatoes, Ma'am?" I whispered again and again. Not once did any of them turn to look at me. Even Miss Richenda paid no attention. Most often I was dismissed by ladies of wasp-like waists with a flap of the hand behind their heads. It was only my quick reactions that saved me from being slapped in the face more than once. I knew whose fault it would be if my face damaged their manicure.

The election might be a foregone conclusion, but the room was abuzz with excitement as they awaited the formal results. Excitement bubbled within me too, but for a quite different reason. I thought Mr Bertram had overreached himself. I did not believe the Inspector would arrest Mr Richard. But perhaps I could bring him to give himself away?

At that moment Mr Bertram, the lawyer and a very unhappy looking Inspector returned. The lawyer returned to his seat, while Mr Bertram debated with the policeman in a quiet, urgent voice by the door. I could not make out what they were saying over the general level of conversation. The guests, after glancing up to see whether it was a messenger from the returning officer, quickly lost interest.

I had just served the last lady. Another footman, who I did not recognise, was about to serve Mr Richard. I gave a little jerk with my head and stepped up quickly.

"Potatoes, Sir?" I said, in a cold voice in Mr Richard's ear.

The result was the best I could have hoped for. The man jumped out of his chair as if I had stuck him with a pin. All eyes turned to the head of the table. "You!" he cried, pointing at me in a most melodramatic and satisfying manner. "How did you . . . ?" He trailed off, suddenly aware of all eyes on him. There was a deadly hush in the room.

I kept my voice low and polite, as I hoped a shy, wronged servant girl might. "Get out of the wardrobe, Sir? I'm afraid I did not find your sister's closet particularly comfortable. Besides, Mrs Wilson needed my help with Holdsworth missing."

Mr Richard turned wild eyes towards Mrs Wilson. His sister, I noticed, kept hers firmly riveted to her plate, but then her ample frame dictated a hearty appetite. "Mrs Wilson, where is my butler?"

Mrs Wilson came forward out of the shadows. She glided over to Mr Richard with mournful grace.

"Damn fool thing!" exclaimed one male guest jovially. "Losing a butler. Big bloke wasn't he that Holdsworth?" He started at the sight of Mrs Wilson. "Good Gad! Who's that female? She's like some giant crow or spectre at the feast, what? Hahaha!" His female companion nipped him on the wrist. He yelped.

"Mrs Wilson, I asked you a question?"

"Sit down," hissed Miss Richenda. "You're making a spectacular of the evening." She turned her attention to the rest of the table. "Do carry on. My brother has been celebrating heartily . . ."

"Shut up, Richenda. I'm not drunk. Mrs Wilson? I'm asking you for the last time."

"He is unavailable, Sir," Her words were low and her voice as dry and brittle as one of Mrs Deighton's sticks of cinnamon.

"Damn you, woman, that's no answer. If you value your position you will answer me."

"Richard, you're making a scene," implored his sister.

"Mrs Wilson!"

"I regret to inform you, Sir, that Mr Holdsworth has given in his notice. A family crisis, I believe. He left before dinner."

I had no expectation of what happened next. Mr Richard turned and grabbed me roughly by the wrist. The serving dish tumbled from my hands and potatoes cascaded across the floor. He dragged me in front of him. "Someone call the police. Holdsworth is the murderer and this girl is his accomplice."

Mr Bertram started forward, but the Inspector laid a hand on his arm, preventing him. "Now, now, Sir. Let's you and I have a little chat outside, shall we, Sir?"

"Inspector, I demand you arrest this girl!"

"On what grounds, Sir?"

"She is the Butler's accomplice."

"So you're saying the Butler did it?"

"Yes. Yes. Man. For God's sake, get your

men after him. He'll flee the country."

"Er, why exactly, Sir? Why did the Butler murder your cousin and your father?"

"Ask her! She knows it all! She told my sister all about it. Some nonsense about a maid. Richenda, tell them?"

Richenda's gaze didn't lift from her plate. "Sit down, Richard," she said softly. "This isn't any good."

"For God's sake, woman. Tell them!"

"Richard, I will not repeat backstairs gossip in company."

"If you have information pertinent to my enquiry, Miss, then I must ask you to speak up now."

Richenda finally looked up. She met the Inspector's gaze square on and said clearly, "I know of nothing useful to you, Inspector. I am afraid my brother has become carried away by the excitement of the night and his very natural grief over our father's death."

Mr Richard still had me in his grip. At this he flung me from him. I managed to put out my hands to save myself, but I took a nasty bang on the hip. There was a collective intake of breath around the table. I sat up, but stayed down, well out of his reach.

"Richard!" cried Mr Bertram. "That is not done!"

"I should have known you'd be behind it. You and your fancy piece."

The Inspector took in the angry aspect of the brothers. "Now, Sirs, I think this is best taken down to the station."

"Damn it, man. I will not go with you. This is election night. I am celebrating."

"I understand that, Sir, but serious charges have been laid against you."

"By who?"

A red flush crept over the Inspector's face. "Your brother and your family's lawyer."

"Peasbody! Peasbody thinks I murdered Pater!"

The man in the well-worn evening dress slid lower in his seat as if contemplating vanishing under the table.

"I didn't say it was the murder we needed to talk to you about, Sir."

"Well, is it or isn't it, man? What are you wittering about? You're making no sense."

The Inspector's face grew redder. "For your sake, Sir, I have refrained from naming the charges, but if you refuse to help us with our enquiries then I will be forced to arrest you."

Mr Richard picked up a goblet of wine and gulped it. "You're an imbecile, man. The Chief Constable is a friend of mine. Watch your mouth or you'll find yourself back walking the beat."

The Inspector motioned to two policemen, who had quietly appeared by the door. "Sir Richard Stapleford, I am arresting you on suspicion of embezzlement, refusing to help the police with their enquiries in a murder investigation . . ." He looked at Mr Bertram, who nodded. "And," continued the Inspector, "on suspicion of murder of the late Sir Stapleford."

For a tiny moment there was silence and stillness as everyone absorbed what the Inspector had said. Every tongue in the room gave forth. Mr Richard did the worst thing possible. He bolted for the door. The two policemen caught him. "Curse you! I've important friends. You'll not get away with this."

"And neither will you, Sir," said the Inspector with a sudden flash of wit.

As the policemen dragged the struggling man away, a hush fell over the room, once more. I got gingerly to my feet.

"Excuse me," piped up a voice, "only I was told to bring the news direct." A small, ginger-haired child in rough clothes had crept into the room. He was clutching his little cloth cap in his hands and twisting it anxiously. "Me da's the returning officer and he said how yous would want to know at once that Sir Richard's won the seat."

Miss Richenda rose gracefully from her seat.

"Thank you, Tommy. That is welcome news. Mrs Wilson, take the lad to the kitchen for his supper and give him a shilling." Her eyes swept across the faces of her startled guests. "This has been a most eventful evening, but I trust it will all be righted in the end. Until my brother can rejoin us, I suggest we move to the withdrawing room. Even the ladies deserve a brandy tonight!"

A polite ripple of amusement met her comment. The guests, all now thinking once more of their stomachs, moved as a bovine herd towards the other room. Mr Bertram came up to me.

"He won't get away with it, will he?" I asked.

He smiled at me. "At the very least, he will be charged with embezzlement. And the city takes that as seriously as murder if not more so!"

I lowered my voice. "You didn't say anything about Holdsworth."

"Apparently, he had already quit the house. A premonition, perhaps?" I suddenly noticed a speck of dust on my shoe. Mr Bertram coughed and continued, "Now he is out of the family's service, I feel no compunction to do the police's work for them."

"You're letting him go?"

Mr Bertram sighed. "Why is it women can never let things be understood, but insist on making matters explicit?"

"We have tidy minds?" I ventured.

He laughed. "That's one term for it."

I felt the tension slipping away from my shoulders as I relaxed for the first time since I arrived. "I am so glad this is over."

"There's going to be a bally mess to clear up," said Mr Bertram ruefully. He ran his hand through his hair. "There's something I need to ask. I wasn't that fair to you earlier. I don't always handle my emotions well. I apologise for my anger. I blame myself for the danger – for Dickie," he broke off, shaking his head as he contemplated the actions of his half-brother. Then he took a resolute breath and continued. "You've been a great help. All fire and guts, as my father would have said."

I felt the heat rush to my face.

"Anyway, I feel I've gotten to know you pretty well during all of this. And whatever else you are, Euphemia, you're smart and you're honourable and you're loyal."

My heart gave a little lurch as I looked up into his earnest face.

"So I have something to ask you." His face split into a grin and he looked suddenly very much younger. "I'm really hoping you'll say yes."

"Well, ask me then and find out," I said. I could feel my own lips curling in response. Everything else faded away. The expression on his face wiping out the nightmare of the past few days.

"Euphemia."

"Yes," I whispered.

"Euphemia, you're not meant to be a maid."

"No?"

"No. I want you to stay on, but as my . . ." he paused and suddenly I believed white knights did rush in to save the day.

"I want you to stay on as my secretary."

"Oh."

"I'll double, no, triple your wages. I'll see Richenda doesn't bother you. I need you, Euphemia. I need someone smart in my corner."

Of course, he did. And I needed the money for Little Joe's schooling. It didn't matter that it felt as if there was a lead weight in my chest where my heart had once been.

"Of course, Sir. I'd be honoured."

Mentally, I reminded myself that the match really would not have done. Socially, Mr Bertram Stapleford ranked much lower than the granddaughter of an Earl. One day I would tell him who I really was, but only when my station was of no consequence to either of us.

I may have mentioned I am a romantic. I should add that despite my mother's efforts to rid me of my whimsy, I remain my father's daughter, and thus one who holds faith in the future.

Author's Notes

Thank you for buying this book and joining
Euphemia on her adventures. I hope you had as
much fun reading her story as I had writing it.

I wanted to write a very different kind of crime
novel. I've always loved reading crime stories,
but I do enjoy the puzzle rather than some of the
more grizzly details. Also, although it feels like
a hundred years ago now, I trained and practised
as a psychotherapist, so it's the motivations and
emotions of people that fascinate me. I don't have
a lot of interest in police procedure, so I wanted
a protagonist who wasn't heavily involved with
the police.

Euphemia is young and with that comes a dose of naïvety. Inspired by her clerical father she believes the very best of people, so coming up against the inhabitants of Stapleford Hall is a bit of a shock.

It was important to me that I created a character who could grow, but was strong enough that all that was good and honest about her would remain in spite of the misfortunes life has thrown at her. She's feisty and courageous and sometimes makes the most foolish of mistakes, but you know it's always for the right reasons, so you can't help rooting for her to come through.

But Euphemia could never have managed to solve the mystery alone, so I gave her Bertram. They need each other. He is much more worldly wise than her, but he's an idealist, who tends to see everything in the terms of grand schemes. He needs Euphemia to bring him down to earth and she needs his understanding of the wider world, of which she knows so little.

The idea of a young woman choosing to go into service is based on something that actually happened in my family. I'm not related to any Earls (as far as I know), but according to family legend, my great grandmother fell out terribly with her father's second wife. It was so bad that her father told her to either make friends with her step-mother or leave. So she left! Her family were very well off with big houses and lots of servants, but she left without a penny and went into service. Like Euphemia she found this very hard, but unlike Euphemia she wasn't strong enough to deal with the very hard work most servants had to do. She fell ill, but somehow – and I don't know the details of the story – she fell in love with my great grandfather and he took her away to run a tobacconist shop together. She never went back to her own family and she was never rich again, but I like to think she was happy.

When I'm writing a story I like to entertain my readers. I enjoy conjuring up worlds and characters, but I also like to make people laugh. Euphemia's world is moving towards a time of great darkness. So her story has to be a balance between light and dark. The Staplefords' world is one of great privilege, but a lot of their wealth is based on arms traders and morally dubious deals. 1910s can be a very idealised time, but not everyone was invited to the party and it's easy to forget that. I've tried to keep Euphemia's story light and funny, but not at the cost of completely ignoring the darker side of those times. After all, courage and laughter in the face of darkness makes for the most heroic of heroines.

Book Club Questions for Discussion

1. Euphemia expects her mother to be very angry when she finally reveals she has a position as a maid, but her mother confuses her by embracing her. Why do you think she behaves like this?

2. Do you like Sergeant Davies? Why? Do you think he's on Euphemia's side?

3. Who ransacked Euphemia's room and what were they looking for?

4. What do you think Bertram's emotions are finding a servant, who both stands up to him and challenges him?

5. Do you think Bertram was right to stay under his father's roof even though he knew how his father earned money and he had enough of his own to move away?

6. Why do you think he did stay?

7. Richenda claims to have political leanings. What are these and do you think she espouses any of these ideals?

8. Why is Sir Stapleford pleased with the way Euphemia deals with the man in the garden? And why is Mrs Wilson cross about it?

9. The Inspector doesn't know the difference between a Bolshevik and a Marxist, do you?

10. When Euphemia realises what Bertram was implying when he said her origins lay her open to temptation she is very cross. Why? What did he mean?

11. Thanks to her father's liberal education Euphemia is more than capable of thinking for herself and is drawn to Richenda's ideas of suffragettism. After all, Euphemia is always very keen for her opinion to be heard! When did British women get the right to vote? Why do you think it happened?

12. Richard behaves towards Euphemia in vastly differing ways. What do you think he feels about her?

13. How does Euphemia work out who wrote the note she finds in the kitchen grate?

14. Why do you think Richenda helps Richard? Why do you think she stops helping him when he appeals to her to back up his story in front of the police?

15. What does Euphemia fear Holdsworth is about to do when she confronts him with the truth? What does he actually do?

16. What does Richard predict right at the very end of the story? Do you think it will happen?

17. Who do you think is smarter Euphemia or Bertram and why?

18. Bertram and Euphemia have very different skills and attitudes that they bring to this investigation. Can you sum up what each of them uniquely offers?

19. Technically Euphemia is of a superior social standing to Bertram, being the granddaughter of an Earl, but knowing her only as a servant he believes her to be below his social standing and does not consider her his equal. Do you think Bertram is being foolish to place so much emphasis on social class? Do you think social class still exists today?

20. There are many differences between life in 1910 and life today. If you could choose, what aspects of that period would you like to see again today and what are you glad we left behind?

A New Euphemia Martins Mystery
Publication date May 2010

A Death in the Highlands

Caroline Dunford

When Euphemia finds herself heading up the female
staff at a hunting lodge in the Highlands of Scotland, she
thinks her biggest challenge is going to be getting along
with the local staff who have a mysterious grudge against
the Staplefords. However, when the guests start to arrive,
Euphemia begins to suspect not everyone is quite who
they seem.
It's not long before Euphemia finds herself at the
heart of a murder mystery that will have international
ramifications.
Peril upon peril abounds and Euphemia will only have her
quick wits and loud scream to protect herself. Especially
as Bertram is being unhelpful and pig-headedly difficult.
Fortunately, there is a sharp-witted, young and rather
handsome new butler to aid her enquiries, but when he is
arrested for the murder, Euphemia is determined to prove
him innocent. In fact almost as determined as Bertram is
to stop her interfering.

ISBN 978-1-905637-95-9   £6.99

ePRINT
PUBLISHING

This Fragile Life

David Webb

Matt felt sick. He sank down onto a chair, the phone still clasped to his ear. He didn't speak for a few moments and Meg broke the silence.
'Are you still there, Matt? Are you all right? I thought you'd want to know.'
'Yes, thanks Meg. I'm coming in. I'm on my way.'
Matt put the phone down and sat still in the dark. Meg's words were echoing in his head and he was desperately trying to make sense of them . . .

Matthew Hudson is constantly reminded just how fragile life can be. Depressed by his routine existence in Manchester, Matt is haunted by the one failed relationship he has behind him – with Lydia, a dancer who left him to further her career in London. However, when he meets Laura, an attractive young primary school teacher, life seems to be looking up for Matt – until one phone call changes everything . . .

This Fragile Life is the first novel produced by prolific children's author David Webb.

ISBN 978-1-905637-87-4   £6.99

PRINT
PUBLISHING

Missing Link

Elizabeth Kay

Spliff laughed softly. "Perhaps outright murder is the only thing we'll stop at on Missing Link. Because just when you all think it can't get any worse, it does . . ."

Jessica Pierce is a guest on the investigative chatshow *Missing Link*. The hugely popular programme is hosted by Spliff, a quick-thinking media-savvy presenter.
The show features two guests; they will never have met before. But a "heaven or hell" link between them is revealed – either something wonderful, such as a long-lost relative, or something appalling, like a false identity.
Spliff violently disapproves of the way television has been dumbed down and he decides to make a programme which will be so shocking that the series will be taken off the air, questions will be asked, and maybe television will be the better for it.
So when Spliff decides to go out with a bang, who will he take with him? . . .

"*Missing Link* teases you, tempts you to think you're as smart as the programme makers who manipulate, backbite and play out cut-throat rivalries behind the scenes. Just when you think you've got its measure—as tart satire on mass entertainment, as comedy of manners, even as romance—it opens a trapdoor on dizzying questions of science and morality. Like its enigmatic and dark-edged romantic lead, Elizabeth Kay's prescient novel layers its witty and intricate mind games with a heartfelt indignation, and even a hint of human vulnerability."
Philip Gross, Author

A skilled and ingenious piece of work
Fay Weldon, Author

ISBN 978-1-905637-88-1   £6.99

PRINT
PUBLISHING

Spectacles

Pippa Goodhart

*For days after that it was as if I'd died and gone to
Heaven. The world was so full of beauty! . . . Seeing the
world so clear felt like falling in love all over again . . .*

When her domineering Mother dies, Iris is shocked by
what she finds when clearing out her flat. It turns out that
she is illegitimate. So Iris isn't the person she'd thought
she was. Perhaps she can reinvent herself now?

When Iris acquires a pair of spectacles, she gains a
renewed focus on life. She gives us her vision of the world
around her, a clear, sometimes almost painfully comic
view of people, places and the Meaning of Life! This
complicated old woman shares some episodes from her life
that move from gentle humour and pure farce to moments
of tragedy and deep despair. Iris is always full of surprises,
and she leaves the biggest surprise till the end of the novel,
when she shocks the reader with the most poignant, eye-
opening revelation of all.

**Throughout this potpourri of a novel, Goodhart writes
with humour and pathos as we follow this wonderful
old woman [...] on an emotional journey.**
Alan Wright, Author, nominated for *Debut Dagger* Award

**A moving story of life, death and all the questions in
between.** Louise Heyden, Librarian

ISBN 978-1-905637-86-7   £6.99

ePRINT
PUBLISHING

A Measure of the Soul

Stephanie Baudet

*The phone rang. Sighing, she went
back into the hall and picked it up,
lifting the earpiece to her ear.*

'Hello?'

*'I see they didn't find him,' said a voice.
'You obviously have him well hidden.'*

Harriet gasped. 'Who is this?' [. . .]

*'Did you really think you could hide
a deserter? How naïve you are,
Miss Baker.'*

For Harriet Baker, looking after her ailing father is a
distressing burden but after his death she is faced with more
problems and must cope alone.

It is 1918, the final year of the Great War, and when her
brother, Alex, goes missing while on compassionate leave,
she fears he will be shot for desertion.

Harriet hides him while the police search the house, never
sure just how he will react in his shell-shocked state,
and when he is seen by others, she is forced to yield to
blackmail and can confide in no-one, not even her best
friend, Gwen...

ISBN 978-1-905637-89-8   £6.99

PRINT
PUBLISHING